STAYING THIN FOR DADDY

For Niamh

Deirdre Brennan

STAYING THIN FOR DADDY

ARLEN
HOUSE

Staying Thin for Daddy

is published in 2014 by
ARLEN HOUSE
42 Grange Abbey Road
Baldoyle
Dublin 13
Ireland
Phone: +353 86 8207617
Email: arlenhouse@gmail.com
arlenhouse.blogspot.com

ISBN 978–1–85132–108–7

International distribution by
SYRACUSE UNIVERSITY PRESS
621 Skytop Road, Suite 110
Syracuse, New York
USA 13244–5290
Phone: 315–443–5534/Fax: 315–443–5545
Email: supress@syr.edu
www.syracuseuniversitypress.syr.edu

Typesetting by Arlen House
Cover artwork by Elizabeth Cope
'Woman in Green with Man in Background'
oil on canvas

CONTENTS

ACKNOWLEDGEMENTS

'The Banana Banshee' was previously published in *Twisted Truths* (Cló Iar-Chonnacht, 2011).

Some of these stories or versions of them have been previously published in *The Irish Times, Passages, Anois, Lá, Comhar, Feasta, Foinse*. Some have been broadcast on RTÉ Radio 1 and Cork Campus Radio.

My thanks to Elizabeth Cope for her lovely cover image from her original painting 'Woman in Green with Man in Background'.

STAYING THIN FOR DADDY

The Tamarisk Trees

This morning I re-read for the first time in months the diary of those days when we honeymooned in Crete. It is not your normal diary of secret thoughts and confidences but rather a series of notes to jog the memory at a later date. The notes themselves are scant. I know the lines by heart. I have sieved them so often for any indication of love or joy or even the person I was then, but I can find none.

And yet I remember there were times in that extraordinary idyll of those early days in Agios Nikolaos when we lay like gods under the shade of the tamarisk trees and the earth unrolled carpets of herbs and wild flowers that seemed to stretch to where horizons shimmered and stirred with our excitement. The diary entry for those days reads:

Dittany; Pot marjoram; Lavender.

Was I unknowingly being cagey? Holding back? Certainly with hindsight it seems likely that I was trying to distance myself even then.

The next entry reads somewhat differently:

> Clay model of a Protogeometric shrine in which there sits a goddess with raised arms, while two males look down from the roof.

I have drawn a small sketch in the margin, probably with a view to using it in my job as a design artist. Beneath that entry I have scrawled in a barely-legible hand:

> Priest wearing animal skins pouring blood libations. Sacred tree and altar in foreground.

Again there is a sketch. This time quite detailed. I never used either of them. The last entry says simply:

> Wild cat amidst lush vegetation preparing to pounce on a pheasant which sits unsuspectingly on a rock.

It was such a lovely cat, such a typical cat-pose. I spent a long time staring at his tense whiskers, his camouflaged body stalking the centuries. There was no need of a sketch or a photograph to remind me. Impulsively I turned to share my find with Alan, but he was nowhere in sight. A sea of Japanese and German tourists milled around me. The best policy was to stay put and he would find me.

That was the Saturday at the end of our first week in Crete and Alan and I had spent most of the day in Heraklion Museum principally to give him a break from the sun which was causing a skin allergy. Not that the allergy was too distressing but he didn't want it to spoil our holiday by worsening his condition. A day out of the sun should see him right. Alan with his fair skin and auburn hair was no sun-worshipper and indeed was most careful to use a high factor sun-block so we were at a loss to know how he ran into any trouble.

We had actually planned to join a tour to Knossos that morning and Alan was insistent that I go without him. Naturally I wouldn't think of it as we had another full week ahead of us and could explore the site together at a later date.

The two of us hadn't exactly rushed into marriage. We had lived together in a flat in Hammersmith for three years before we took the plunge. From time to time we had spoken of tying the knot, but always in a joking way. I was wary of doing the pushy woman bit although I felt that once men get past thirty they get a bit set in their ways. I myself was twenty five and reckoned it was time to be serious.

It was Alan who brought up the subject sometime before Christmas when we were about to travel to Ireland for the holidays.

'You know, Emma', he said casually, 'I think we ought to get hitched and have done with it'.

Just like that. I was over the moon. I was crazy about the guy. We had never been happier. An antique sapphire glowed our love from my left hand and the date was settled for a June wedding.

I was planning that we should get married in London or perhaps on the beach in Antigua. My parents were conventional Irish Catholics and weren't taking too kindly to the idea of their only daughter marrying an Englishman with no religion at all. At least if we kept away from home the parents would not have to explain the situation to relations and friends. Antigua appeared to be the best bet. It would sound colourful and splendidly exotic. I could hear my folks' bravado.

'Emma's so unconventional you know. No doubt she'll wear a grass skirt'.

'But you'll surely travel out for the wedding?'

'Not a chance of it. How could we leave the farm at this time of year? But we'll have a bit of an old party when they come over'.

We were washing our red Mazda one Sunday morning when Alan said casually as could be, 'I'm thinking of converting'.

'Converting?' I swabbed away. 'Do you mean to gas?'

'Don't be a twit, Emma. To Roman Catholicism'.

'You're kidding. What the hell would you do that for?' I was totally flummoxed.

'Well you know, if we have children it'll make life simpler. I thought you'd be pleased', he said.

'Are you having me on?' I asked.

'No. I'm dead serious'.

'But, for God's sake, Alan, what put that in your head? I mean you know my feelings. I'm a lapsed Catholic. I'd hate you to think you were being pressurised by me in any way'.

Before I knew where I was, the flat was full of religious books, bibles, old papal encyclicals on marriage, histories of the Church and the Christian mystics. Alan was never one for half measures. He talked to me incessantly about religion. Religion in my childhood, in my family, in my school. All the images and associations I wanted to forget were dredged up again, the doctrines that I felt had stifled me. I feared too that Alan was becoming a religious bore. I could see the glazed eyes of our friends at dinner parties when he started expounding on transubstantiation in the middle of our hostess' chocolate roulade or lemon soufflé. And I wasn't at all sure how he could have so suddenly got hung up on Christ. Maybe it was because he had had no religious instruction whatever, maybe it was because he was heading for thirty three that year and felt an instant empathy with all thirty somethings. Whatever it was he was now taking instruction from Father Cyril, a Jesuit who was in London on a sabbatical from San Francisco. Apparently he was researching a treatise on Saint Teresa of Avila.

'You'll have to meet Cyril, he's wonderfully interesting', Alan enthused, 'and he's simply dying to meet you'.

I'll just bet he is, I thought sourly. A fisher of souls ready to yank me back into the net. But I held my peace.

Cyril's place was in a quiet cul de sac within walking distance from us. I remember well the Sunday afternoon when I first visited him with Alan. The house was quite misleading. The facade was that of a typical period red-bricked Victorian house. Inside someone had done a ghastly conversion job. Ceilings had been lowered and the rooms fitted out in the worst possible taste with tatty nondescript furniture, beige sisal flooring and drab curtains. The sink and cooker were disguised as a wardrobe. The back window had been fitted with bars for security reasons since it was a ground floor flat. A watery winter sun cast their shadows along the floor giving the impression of a cage.

I always think that people's possessions tell you so much about themselves. Clearly the priest had travelled lightly. There were no photographs, no pictures, no bric-a-brac. Not even a crucifix for God's sake! Just rows and rows of books on metallic office shelving to the right of the cast iron fireplace. By the main window which looked out on the street was a cheap wooden table functioning as a desk. There was no clutter whatever on it. A laptop was positioned to one side with some neatly stacked papers. That was it.

'How long have you lived here?' I asked

'Just eighteen months', was the reply.

It was hard to understand how anyone could live in such a pad all those months and leave no stamp of ownership. It seemed to me that Alan and I were quite out of place there. I thought of our own bright airy flat, Alan's glass collection with the light shining through it; the squashy comfortable sofa with colourful ethnic throws and the lingering smell of spices from the kitchen.

In some strange way I began to feel sorry for Father Cyril cooped up in this cell and some of the antagonism drained from me.

'So how's the conversion going, Father?' I smiled warmly.

'It's Cyril', he said, 'but I've no work to do at all. I merely guide Alan's reading'.

'You do that alright', Alan laughed happily.

The priest was in his late thirties, tall, thin and athletic in his movements. He produced a bottle of Californian wine from a small fridge that was disguised as a cupboard.

'I guess I have to be patriotic', he smiled. 'I've been to the winery in Santa Cruz where this bottle hails from. I hope you like it Emma'.

'*Ní i Santa Cruz d'fhágfainn mo chnámha faoin bhfód*', I murmured tasting it.

'Is that Gaelic?' he asked.

'Yes, but I have the wrong Santa Cruz. I think mine is in South America. The wine is lovely'.

I saw the label on the bottle, *Il Pescatore*. I couldn't keep the smirk off my face. God, talk about subtlety! He spotted my expression. Our eyes met for a fraction of a second.

'It's actually great with seafood', he said lightly.

I noticed how at ease Alan was with him. But then the priest had that laid-back American manner calculated to put one at ease.

I must admit that neither at that meeting nor at any ensuing meeting when I was present was religion ever mentioned and by the time Cyril married us in Ireland in June Alan had grown accustomed to his new faith. That is to say he didn't need to talk about it non-stop. By then too, I had grown quite fond of Father Cyril. We had a wonderful wedding. I was glad we did not have to settle for Antigua. It would have been quite lonely without the fussing of family and old friends.

Twenty minutes must have passed since I missed Alan. I was damned if I was going to stand in the middle of the museum with my cat and pheasant for very much longer. Why, oh why, wasn't he coming? How on earth could we have got separated like that? It was completely out of character for him to stray off without as much as a word. I began to worry that the anti-histamine tablets he was taking for his allergy might have made him drowsy and that he had collapsed in the crowds. That armies of Japanese and Germans with their cameras were marching over him as he lay on the ground. That he had passed out in the men's toilets with nobody to help him. I could feel myself drown in waves of panic. There had to be a logical explanation. A man six feet tall does not vanish. My eyes panning over the crowds, I struggled to the main entrance to have Alan paged. To my amazement when I reached the desk there he was with a worried look on his face and beside him in shorts and a baseball hat was, of all people, Cyril! They saw me instantly. Alan put his arms around me in relief.

'Where the hell did you get to', he chastised. 'We were just having you called on the PA system'.

All I could do was laugh semi-hysterically.

It emerged that Cyril had taken a flight cancellation to Malia, never for an instant thinking that he would run into us since our destination had been a well-kept secret. He just could not believe his good luck. We explained to him that we were returning to our hotel in Agios Nikolaus and would have to run immediately or we would miss our tour bus.

'You should come and spend a day with us', I told him. 'It's a fantastic place'.

'So is Malia', he laughed.

Cyril took up our invitation and came to visit us the following Tuesday. In the morning we lay under the shade of the tamarisk trees that edged the shore and we swam and talked for hours. Later we brought Cyril to a taverna we had discovered that served the most marvellous stuffed vine leaves and souvlaki that you would sell your soul for. We sat at a table near the open door where bunches of grapes, greenly pellucid in the evening light, dangled over the lintel.

Maybe I drank too much retsina or took too much sun during the day. Maybe it was a combination of both. I do not know. But suddenly I felt an unease I could not put words on. It was absolutely irrational. The talk of the men fluttered past me and an unaccustomed sadness welled up in me. I watched the mosquitoes gather around the lights.

'Are you alright, Emma?' questioned Cyril. 'You're very quiet'.

'Of course', I turned to him with a perplexed smile and then banished the moment from me.

Cyril managed to get a room in our hotel for the night and planned to return to Malia the following day.

Whatever strange feeling or premonition that disturbed me the previous evening was totally gone by morning. I rose about eight thirty leaving Alan fast asleep and wrote a note telling him that I had gone to the market to buy some pieces of pottery to take home as souvenirs and that I would be back for coffee, at the earliest, around eleven.

On my way out through the back entrance of the hotel I saw Cyril in the distance diving into the swimming pool. I recognised the distinctive leopard skin print of his bathing trunks. For a moment, unseen by him, I watched his stylish crawl up the pool and then I turned and passed under the awning of bougainvillea which led onto the street.

The morning was fresh and abuzz with activity. Housewives and tourists were already lining up at the bakery for fresh bread and baklavas. The sticky almondy pastries smelled so enticing I bought three for our morning coffee. After that it was no time until I reached the market and made my purchases. I wandered down some narrow side streets where old women clad in black were sitting in shady doorways crocheting lace and keeping an eye on some toddlers at play. They showed no interest whatever in me although I would have been happy to have stopped and talked. Already it was getting very warm. My pottery and pastries were growing heavier by the minute so despite the fact that it was not quite ten o'clock I decided to return to the hotel.

I turned the key of our bedroom door very quietly intending to surprise Alan if he was awake or not disturb him if he was still sleeping. Then I stopped in my tracks transfixed. My mouth opened and I was sure my scream filled the room. Later I realised that no sound came.

Cyril was in bed with my husband. Their lovemaking was so intense they were not even aware of my presence. I felt a great ocean roaring in my head. My skin burned with an intolerable heat. The sweet smell of the baklavas was nauseating. I could not breathe and I dared not look again. My eyes dropped to the black and white tiled floor where the leopard skin trunks lay triumphantly splayed.

Translated by the author

THE BANSHEE

I was eleven and small for my age the summer that Molly came to live with us. We were poor because my father had been out of work since he strained his back two years before I was born. Mother ran a boarding house to make ends meet. At first she took summer visitors and later when she got established, we had guests for most of the year. It was very hard work. That is why she needed Molly.

You couldn't call Molly a maid. Only posh people had maids. You'd see them down in Atlantic Terrace polishing the front door brasses early in the mornings and then hanging up striped covers on the doors before the sun could blister the varnish. These maids wore uniforms. Before lunch they wore starched white caps and black dresses with plain white aprons. In the afternoons when they answered the doors to callers they had changed the plain aprons for frilly ones and wore little lacy white mobcaps on their hair. I knew all this because sometimes when my mother ran me out of the house and I drifted around aimlessly with nothing to do, I used to ring the door-bells in Atlantic Terrace and pretend to be looking for the Warrens or any other name that came into my head. I loved staring inside their houses. They were so gleaming and mysterious compared to ours.

Molly was different to the terrace maids. She used to wear a flowery overall that wrapped around and tied in a bow at the back. She was a big strapping island girl with black curly hair and grey eyes and a pink and white skin like the Irish Colleen dolls in the souvenir shop. She was very good-humoured and hardly ever chased me out of the kitchen the way my mother did. I was well used to Mother grumbling.

'Will you get the hell out of my sight Declan! Why don't you go out and play? A big boy like you stuck in a book on a summer's day!'

It seemed to irritate my father too any time he saw me around the house. He used to attack my mother.

'For God's sake will you stop mollycoddling that lad! Out playing games he should be instead of stuck inside with a pair of women'.

'Isn't it a fierce pity', she used to retort, 'that you couldn't spend a little more time around the place yourself. Believe me, I could find work in plenty for you. You're nothing but a layabout. That's what you are'.

I used to feel embarrassed with them squabbling in front of Molly but she always acted as if she never heard. I suppose my mother was right. Father was a layabout. He had a built-in radar system that warned him off when work was being done. He spent his days with his cronies chatting up visitors along the sea front or in the bookies listening to the races on radio. Most nights he spent in the local cadging drinks from tourists or he might go to a neighbour's house for a hand of poker. One thing was certain. He took on a different personality the minute he closed our front gate behind him.

Once I met him in the corner shop where I had been sent on a message. I couldn't believe my eyes. There was Father cracking jokes and acting them out. He was really very funny. Mary, the shop assistant and two customers were simply falling around the place laughing at him.

'God, you're a howl Billy! There's no doubt about it, you should be on the stage!' said Mary wiping away her tears with the back of her hand.

I stood there gaping, not believing that this was the same man who lived with us. He turned and saw me and kept up the act.

'Ah, there you are Declan, *a mhic!* What'll it be?'

He put his arm around my shoulders. I was flabbergasted.

'He's lost his tongue', Father joked. 'Give us a quarter of Cleeve's toffees for the boy, Mary'. And winking, he pressed the little paper bag into my fist.

Molly began to settle down and become part of the family. The mornings were spent making the beds, cleaning, tidying and preparing the vegetables for dinner at one o'clock. We had four Christian Brothers staying with us. Mother said they were no bother really. They weren't at all fussy about their food and were most appreciative of whatever was put in front of them. I heard her talking to her friend Mrs. O'Connor.

'All they want is good plain food. If you dressed the chops in egg and breadcrumbs they would just scrape it off!'

'Aren't you loaded with luck Nancy!' said Mrs O'Connor. 'I've this couple for a fortnight with three spoiled brats who turn up their noses at stewed apples and custard. Now I ask you!'

The Christian Brothers spent their time out walking or swimming up at the rocky end of the strand. In the evenings they sat in the parlour reading newspapers and smoking.

When the house was full of visitors Mother moved Molly and ourselves out to a big hut in the back garden. This hut was rather grandly called the 'Bungalow'. Molly had a few hours off every afternoon when the clearing up was done after dinner. Sometimes she used to ask me to go for a walk with her. I liked that because we generally stopped at the ice-cream kiosk close to the strand and she would buy us vanilla wafers. Other times we used to wander around Pipers' Amusements and ride in the bumpers. I knew that Molly was lonely because she told me she missed her family and life on the island. There were six children in their house.

'We've great gas at home', she told me, 'not like you lot. I don't know how your Ma stands it. Sure all she thinks of is the work. Some life!'

'But if you have six children in your house', I protested, 'your mother must work very hard too'.

'Divil a bit of it', she said. 'We wouldn't have your fine ways'.

'Will you bring me to the island sometime?' I begged.

'Why not if your Ma lets you!'

I nearly burst with excitement. I'd never been away anywhere.

By the end of June the first Christian Brothers had returned home and four others came to take their place. One of them was a tall, pale, weedy-looking young man called Brother Wall. He had come to convalesce, according to my mother, and was going to stay for a month longer than his companions. She was being paid well to look after him and build up his strength. When the others were having their elevenses of tea and Marietta biscuits in the front garden, Brother Wall sat in the parlour lest he catch a chill and Mother sent Molly in with egg-flip to him. She had instructions to stand over him until he drained the last drop.

After a fortnight you could see the improvement in him. He began to put on weight and his walks along the prom got a little longer every day. Molly and he used to joke and banter together. I gave him a wide berth as he was usually ready with a problem in mental arithmetic for me. I imagine how he must torture his pupils in school if he couldn't lay off me in the summer holidays.

'Come here Declan', he would call, showing off to Molly. 'Suppose you are trying to fill a bath with water and it takes fifteen gallons to fill the bath. Now if the stopper is defective and the water leaks out at the rate of one pint a minute, how long would it take to fill the bath if the water is flowing in from the taps at the rate of three pints a minute?'

I didn't like his line in conversation. Molly annoyed me too. She needn't have laughed at his silly jokes. Maybe I was a bit jealous. She didn't bring me walking any more.

One day when I wandered into the Amusement Park I spotted the two of them in the bumpers. It was clear to me that Brother Wall thought he was a rally driver as he twisted the steering wheel this way and that, trying to avoid the other bumpers. Why get into the bumpers at all if he didn't want to bump? Still Molly seemed to be enjoying herself. Her cheeks were bright pink and she was screeching and laughing.

I slipped away in case they would see me. Another time, I came upon the two of them paddling in a little rock pool. He had his black pants rolled up above his knees. I noticed his white graveyard legs. Molly's red dirndl skirt was soaking wet. They were laughing and splashing each other like a pair of babies. I just couldn't believe that people of their age could be so foolish.

By the second week of August Brother Wall had said goodbye, promising to come again next year if not sooner. Molly was very quiet when he left and went off on her own when the washing-up was done.

'She'll miss the young company', said my mother to Mrs O'Connor when she called in later that evening.

'No harm at all he's gone', Mrs O'Connor replied. 'I'd say the Brothers wouldn't like to know that he was so pally with a young girl'.

'Sure 'twas nothing but a bit of innocence', said my mother. 'It took the poor lad out of himself'.

The following week, the weather broke and the green striped deckchairs were stashed away under the stairs as rainy day followed rainy day and we knew the summer wouldn't come back. Business was bad. There had been two cancellations. Father, Mother and I moved back into the house and Molly stayed on in the bungalow.

'You should give that girl her walking papers', said my father. 'There isn't enough work for her to do around here with the season as good as over'.

'I haven't a notion of it', said my mother. 'I'm going to advertise for year-round lodgers in September. Molly is reliable. I mightn't get as good again'.

Father was livid. You could see the way he worked himself up until the veins stood out over his shirt collar.

'Is a man never to have a bit of peace at his own fireside? Have I always to be tripping over strangers? Is there never any consideration for me? Tell me that?'

Mother had a sad resigned look on her face. 'You know perfectly well we need the money', she said.

Father put on his felt hat and banged the door after him. The china on the dresser rattled. We didn't see him again until tea-time. He was always on the dot for his meals.

A postcard came from Brother Wall. He was feeling great and ready to tackle the school year. Molly got a letter from him. I knew it was from him even though her name and address was printed. Besides, she never got a letter at our house before. She stuffed it into her apron pocket and didn't read it until she was in the bungalow on her own. She got two more letters from him before Christmas. After that I lost interest in herself and Brother Wall because we had three girls lodging with us. Two of them were secretaries and one was a bank clerk in the town. They spent their time coming and going. I used to run errands for them fetching them cigarettes and magazines from the corner shop. I missed them when they went home for the Easter holidays.

The house seemed so lonely and dull without them. Molly went around with a long face. She was no fun any more.

'Take the week off, Molly', said my mother. 'You haven't seen your family for an age now and it's grand and slack here at the moment'.

'You might need me yet ma'am', she answered. 'Didn't the Brothers say that they might come for a few days around the Easter?'

'That was only talk at the time, Molly. You go back to your folks. I don't know what they'll think of you. You're so pale. Indeed you're as bad as Declan now. Always stuck in the house'.

Molly was pouring tea for my father from the big aluminium teapot when I noticed a slight gasp and saw her stiffen. Then she continued to pour as if nothing had happened. The radio beeped for the ten o'clock night news.

'I'll be going now ma'am', said Molly.

'You'll have a sup of tea first', said Mother.

'No, thanks all the same. I'll see you in the morning'.

She lifted the latch on the back door and Mother drew the bolt across.

'I'll have an early night myself', she yawned, 'don't you be up too late Declan'.

When I went to bed, I read for a long time. It was a mystery thriller and I couldn't put it down. My bedroom was a small one at the back of the house. The bed was rammed in between the door-wall and a window that overlooked the bungalow in the garden. I was aware of the wind rising and the lonely moan it made in the buoy far out in the bay. Just before settling down for the night, I pulled the curtains aside. The light was still on in the bungalow. I was watching clouds blowing across the face of the moon when I heard a baby scream. It seemed very near. I got out of bed and tiptoed downstairs. Groping my way through the dark kitchen, I reached the back door when I heard it again. It was a loud cry. Suddenly it stopped. It had to be in our garden. I shot back the bolt on the kitchen door and feeling the cold cement steps under my bare feet I headed down the garden towards the bungalow.

'Molly!' I called.

There was no answer. I knocked on the window, noticing that it was open a few inches on top. I climbed up on the window sill and shouted through the opening.

'Molly, did you hear something?'

'Go away Declan'. I recognized Molly's voice although it was sort of hoarse.

'Let me in Molly', I pleaded.

There was no sound from the bungalow. I tried again.

'Molly, I heard a baby crying. It must be somewhere in the garden'.

She didn't answer. I jumped down off the sill.

Suddenly her face appeared at the window. It looked queer in the moonlight as if the glass distorted it in some way, like the crazy mirrors down at the Amusements.

'I heard a baby Molly ...' I started.

'You heard the Banshee', she gasped. 'She's coming for you, Declan. Now go back to your bed or she'll catch you'.

I turned away. I didn't believe in the Banshee. My mother said that she was just like giants and ghosts made up to scare people. So, I searched our small patch of garden on my own in the moonlight and found nothing.

The following morning when I got up, Molly was buttering thick chunks of bread. Her face was pale and drawn. Her dark curly hair was tied back from it with a red ribbon. She was wearing a freshly-ironed navy overall patterned with tiny blue flowers. She looked at me straight in the eye.

'Sit down and don't be gaping Declan', she said. 'You must be starving after your night ramblings'.

I dropped my eyes from hers. I never heard that baby cry again.

Translated by the author

CHER ANTOINE

They say your whole life flashes in front of you when you are about to die. Mine did. Well, up to a point it did, but I kept being diverted by other more riveting images. However, I can say that I saw my life zoom past in overdrive, hitting and running at my childhood, my forlorn adolescence, changing lanes and skidding to a halt to linger on the firm's flashcards with their glib maxims which pin-pointed all my inadequacies:

'Development begins from within'.
'Performance is a fraction of your potential'.
'You unlimited'.

I figured I had good reason to worry. One bad report from Tony and I'd be given the chop. I saw me going nowhere really fast; saw me sitting dismally, like a moulting wren, with all my immoderate aspirations coming to roost in me; saw me beavering away at my desk, plumbing the depths of *me unlimited* and coming up with nothing, not even an old boot. If there was a hell, I'd very likely be condemned to casting such lines forever. Indeed I had no guarantee but the powers that be might relegate me to a similar heaven.

But, as I said, I got diverted from my dying. There I was all thumbs, trying to release a girl's long golden hair which was entangled in the base of the lock gates. The more I tried to unravel the hair the more bound she became. All the time I was aware of the second finger on my left hand throbbing painfully and hovering over us, through the weedy water, the sinister outline of her upturned boat. I was diving, choking, diving, unable to release her.

During this frenzied activity, I realised that there was an inconsistency somewhere. It was niggling away at me as I tried to raise the girl's limp head. Then it flashed across my mind that I was in the water precisely because I couldn't swim. Struggling not to lose my nerve by this realisation, I finally managed to angle her head. Her eyes were wide open and glazed like those of a salmon on a fishmonger's slab. I was looking into my own eyes. This being too horrific an image to dwell on, the face, in an audacious dreamlike fashion, gave way to a blue flower on a cliff face; a flower of intense blue like the cerulean of a Himalayan poppy. I hunted it single-mindedly but it was always in a crevice high beyond my reach. This image was backed by a soundtrack of the strangest, sweetest music. No sharps, no flats, no grace-notes; music of the purest intensity such as lone travellers have been known to hear coming out of caves and openings of the earth. A Lorelei's song of inscrutable, unsurpassable beauty.

Unexpectedly, it was snatched from me. The flower vanished, the music silenced. I was in a baby bath being squeezed and pressed like a child's squeegee starfish until weak jets of water squirted from my rubber lips. Then I was all lips like the lip fountain I had seen with Tony in front of the Pompidou Centre in Paris. Fingers probed my throat searching out detritus, leaves, weeds, cigarette paper. Unblocked, water gushed from my mouth unendingly. My lungs ballooned and somewhere on the edge of consciousness an ambulance sounded.

Tony was beside my hospital bed. I didn't dare open my eyes even though I felt as fizzy as red lemonade with out-and-out relief at being alive. Which, of course, was absurd in so far as I should have been dismayed at having another botched venture on my hands. But why should that worry me? Napoleon himself was a failed suicide. And he used a vial of poison which you'd have sworn was a certainty.

'Why did you do it, Meg? Why? Why?'

I knew from the whinge in Tony's voice that what he really meant was: 'Why did you do it to me?'

Nevertheless, it was quite a good question. Even without looking, I had no difficulty imagining him hunched in the visitor's chair, his eyes downcast behind his thin-rimmed glasses. He had such a sense of drama, his English tinged with a slight French accent inherited, according to him, from his mother. It was those very tones I found fascinating in the first place. He was a trifle fastidious in a superior rather than an effeminate way and would have found it too unbearable to watch me, too unendurable to touch me after what I had done.

'Cher Antoine', I must have murmured audibly, although I could have sworn my lips didn't move.

'Nurse', he shouted. 'Nurse, I think she's coming to'.

I hadn't a notion of coming to, at least not while he was around. How had he got here in the first place? Could I have possibly sent for him when in some doped, sedated state? Talk about screwing things up!

The sweetness and the redness of the lemonade was fading and I now felt more like clear, carbonated water. I tried to concentrate on every bubble while the nurse came and went. It was a bit like counting sheep. They all looked the same but unlike sheep, I couldn't discipline them, couldn't drive them through any gap or channel. They kept laughing and exploding in giddy succession so I lost count.

My finger still pulsed in a festery way. I remembered how it hurt when I was trying to untangle the girl's hair as if each strand were a cheese wire cutting deeply. The kitchen devil had slipped when I was slicing tomato for my last supper. I actually thought of this meal in sacramental terms. The drawing of blood took on a sacrificial significance. I bound the wound ceremonially in pink toilet paper until the bleeding stopped. There was no point in opening a new box of Elastoplasts when I was going to die in the next two hours.

In the beginning Tony was my boss. In the very beginning, he sat on the panel that interviewed me for the job. Later he told me that my interview had been impressive, that he had no doubt that my performance in sales would be likewise. He was dead right. I worked the butt off myself for the firm but in reality it was for him. Idiot that I was this latter truth didn't penetrate until it was too late. It never entered my head that the firm didn't recognise my existence. Tony got all the credit for my work, while I pondered on my performance, keeping my fingers crossed that it was only a fraction of my potential. I had a sneaking suspicion that there was very little else I could trawl from my diminishing shallows.

In previous jobs, my policy had been never to mix business with pleasure. I kept to myself, not socialising with anyone from the workplace. However, the firm believed that if we played as well as worked together we bonded and made a better team. Weekend getaways combining seminars with fun in romantic country castles and Georgian houses all helped the work output and unexpectedly catapulted me into Tony's arms. I was the one who was gormlessly surprised when it happened. We had to keep the affair deadly secret since the firm, although encouraging sociability, did not encourage fraternisation between senior management and subordinates. I had never heard anything more puritanical in my life but Tony insisted it was common policy with American firms, based on a militaristic running of organisations on West Point principles. I was gobsmacked but agreed since both of us, if found out, could lose our jobs.

So Tony came and went, never actually moving in with me nor suggesting I move in with him. He wined me, dined me, said it with flowers. Never with words. He had me eating out of the palms of his thin, manicured hands. More than ever, I was anxious to please him. I was mainly worried that he would discover I was the fraud I knew myself to be. I felt tense and burnt out at work. At home, I was on tenterhooks wondering if he would phone me, if he would ring the doorbell, if he would come at all.

About nine months into our affair, on one of those Sundays when I was thoroughly fed up waiting for some word of him, I decided to blow away the cobwebs with a walk on Dún Laoghaire pier. Let him phone. Let him bang despairingly on my door. Let his florist roses pile high as a mountain on my step. In future I wouldn't be so readily available.

It was a fortuitous trip for who did I spy out walking but Tony with his wife and two small children playing happy families. There and then I wanted to die.

When I tackled him with what I had seen, he gave a Gallic shrug of his shoulders and said, 'Come, come, Meg, don't pretend you didn't know'.

How in God's name would I have known? Yet how could I have been so naïve, so blinkered? As I stood confronting him, I actually heard the scales dropping from my eyes and being scrunched under his retreating feet.

That was when I started calling him *Cher Antoine*. It was a kind of sick little joke to lighten my despair.

My counsellor and I have had long sessions to reconstruct the feelings that compelled me to end it all but I believe I drowned those feelings and I really didn't want to dredge them up.

'You must face them, Meg', he said, 'or you'll very likely try again'.

I explained to him that when I did the deed, I was frozen with despondency. That I could only picture myself as a snowman melting into the Grand Canal. That further living was unthinkable. That now, in my new euphoria, and gratitude for life, I wanted to rejoice, to sing and shout, to ditch Tony and the firm, to sign on for night classes in belly-dancing, to send the two young lads who rescued me on a dream holiday when I could put a few quid together.

'You look yellow, Meg', the counsellor interrupted.

Why not? I felt like a sunflower revelling in summer, or like a cornfield rippling in a golden wind.

'You look yellow, Meg', said the doctor. 'Are you nauseous? We must do some blood tests'.

My friends from the firm visit me most days. They never mention *Cher Antoine*. Chat and laughter brim illogically in me. I talk excitedly as if by talking I can dull my illness.

Yellow is sunshine and gorse and daffodils but yellow is death too. My mind these days goes back to water sleek as a rodent's back. Delicate as its whiskers brushing me. I have contracted Weil's disease from rats' urine in the canal and irony of ironies, if I had used an Elastoplast I might not be about to die a second time. The infection entered my body through my cut finger.

I have taken to wondering if my life will flash in front of me again; if I'll hunt a blue flower, or will it be yellow, if I'll hear the song of the canal Lorelei. It is probably unlikely as I think I've changed in subtle ways. And this time I'll die in a hospital bed.

I wonder will *Cher Antoine* send me funeral roses.

FERN

I never cared for the brat. She was born with the same sulky look as her mother. As to why I got hitched to Rosie in the first place, I'll never know – I suppose a fella did what was expected of him in those days. You could say I was an innocent abroad. A decent Irish yob codded up to the eyeballs by this blond fluffy English one. My mates warned me. Told me that Rosie was out to nab me. So in the heel of the hunt there was only myself to blame.

'Let's call her Fern', she cooed over the brat.

Now, I'd describe myself as an ordinary guy with ordinary down-to-earth views on everything, names included, but Fern was more than I could stomach.

'What about Nancy? That's a nice name', I said, suddenly getting all mushy about the ma back home in Ireland that I hadn't seen for five years. But Fern it was and I got my own back by calling her nothing.

That's one thing about me, nobody fucks me up. Not now, not ever. I remember when I was a young lad I was really fond of horses. There was nothing I liked better than handling them. Moriarty's had this grocer's shop cum pub cum bakery at the corner of the street opposite the Presentation Convent. They owned the picture house up the street as well. But my main interest was the horse that pulled their bread delivery van. A fine chestnut mare with white fetlocks and a splodgy star on her forehead, she was called Dolly. I used to suck up to the bread man so he would sometimes let me put a grain bag around her head and I would stand there stroking her while she munched. One day didn't Mrs Moriarty waddle out of the shop, her hair all permed up and a flowery shop-coat on her.

'Well, Danno', says she, 'so I see you like horses. How would you like to unharness Dolly every evening, brush her down and bring her to the field behind the shop?'

Would I what! Me and the bread man helped each other and then it was off with me to the field. I couldn't get over my good luck when Mrs Moriarty used to reward me with a fistful of sweets from a tall glass jar behind the counter. I remember how the rings on her sausagey fingers glittered amongst the cellophane-covered toffees.

Well I loved horses and I got to thinking that an animal like Dolly should have a bit of proper exercise instead of hauling a bread van day in and day out. This Friday evening up I leapt on her back and good as any gun-totin' Hollywood cowboy I galloped her bareback round and round the field till we were both in a slather. Then I left her to cool off a bit while I headed back to collect my sweets, but wasn't Mrs Moriarty standing at the gate waiting for me.

'Howaya!' says I.

She never spoke a word but drew out and lashed me across the pus with her jewelled hand. When I didn't knock the head off her! The ould bitch. I sniggered in her face. She was some fool if she thought that Danno Carey would take shit from the likes of her. But let her wait!

The next day opportunity knocked. Didn't I spot a lorryload of pigs being dropped off at the piggery in the lane behind the picture house that gave me an idea. I had made it my business to know that the keys to the picture house were kept in the pub beside the Child of Prague statue up on the third shelf behind the counter. I waited until I spotted Mrs M going down town so in I go, cool as a breeze. Fonsie, the barman, was reading the racing results in the *Irish Independent* and looked up dopily.

'Mrs Moriarty sent me for the keys', says I, pointing to the statue behind him.

Like a zombie, he reached them down. After that, it was plain sailing. I led out the pigs one by one and locked all twenty five of them into the picture house. It would have been quicker if I could have herded them all in together, but I reckoned they would have stampeded and given the game away. It was quarter past eight that evening when I saw Mrs M head off to open the box office. A bit of a queue had formed to see *Gone with the Wind*. I joined it and nearly pissed in my pants when I heard the grunting and squealing coming from inside and imagined the pigshit on the new green carpet.

The brat reminded me of those pigs, squealing and snuffling away night and day for the first year. I made myself scarce, I can tell you. Me and the lads met up in The Plough every night. We had great gas and the few pints kept me sane not to talk of the bit of ould guff about Ireland.

Rosie nagged on and on. What kind of a father are you? You ignore the poor child. Would you not put a bit of paint on the room and brighten it up for her? And you could at least take her in her go-car to the park. Do you love us at all, Danno? Do you love us?

I wished to God she'd just shut up. Love, me arse! She didn't know how well off she was. I tied the knot didn't I? Many's the man would have taken to his heels when she got herself in the family way. All I heard was Fern this and Fern that and she's cut another tooth. And guess what Danno? She said Da-da to-day. Isn't she the clever koochie-poochie? Jayze! You could say Rosie and her bloody Fern drove me out of the house. Not a house actually. The three of us were crammed into a small room in Camden Town.

Still, I had a few trump cards up my sleeve. Rosie knew little or nothing about me. Ok, she knew I was Irish. But, she didn't know where I came from or if I had a family or anything. She wasn't all that curious either. Took me as she found me. No cop-on. Even my mates would've known better than to cross me. I told them once how I got my own back on a gang of fellas from Carlow who had done the dirt on me. There was this ould wan who was fond of a drop of port wine. She used to come to town in her pony and trap on a Saturday and she used to let me drive her back the few miles home. I would unload the groceries and look after the pony for her. She had a grand orchard and let me pick whatever apples I wanted.

I let the gang know where there was this great orchard to rob. Everything worked according to plan and I was in the house with the ould wan when I spied the movement in the apple trees.

'Mrs', I shouted, 'there are some lads below robbing the orchard'.

She grabbed her shotgun from beside the Sacred Heart lamp on the high mantel and, quick as a greyhound let loose from her cage, she lunged at the lads, firing shot in all directions. They scattered like the pack of rats they were and boy I fell around the place laughing.

The brat was three and Rosie was working part-time in the corner shop on Lordship Street when I came in worn out from a hard day on the building site. The radio was blaring full blast. My stomach was shaking hands with my backbone but there wasn't as much as a whiff of the steak and onions she had promised. A note on the table said, 'Danno, I've had enough. Me and Fern are moving in with Mehmet'.

Mehmet? Who the bloody hell was Mehmet? Her pimp! Oh the little whore. Didn't I always know she was. She double crossed me with some prick she'd picked up in the corner shop. By Christ I'd show her not to mess with Danno Carey!

Then I had a great stroke of luck. I was sitting in a cafe, tucking into a big breakfast fry-up, the Saturday morning after she took off, when who did I see shimmying along the street but the bould Rosie. No sign of the brat. She was all out in one of those pencil skirts and four-inch heels. I followed at a safe distance, saw her turn down High Street and put a key in a red door.

The following day there was I pressing the bell on the same doorstep. This big greasy Turk opens the door.

'Mehmet, I presume', says I, smooth as you like. 'I'm not looking for a fight. Just calling to bring the child for a walk'.

'Rosie!' he roars, and she comes to the door with the brat trailing after her. She looked very pale and nervous when she saw me.

'I'll bring the young one to the park', says I. 'A child needs her da'.

I didn't think it was going to work and then says she, 'Well, I suppose. But you must have her back by six for tea'.

I had the whole thing worked out like a military operation. A taxi to Euston Station and off we were to Holyhead to catch the night boat to Ireland. I filled the brat with sweets and lemonade and she was full of chat and talk, jumping up and down with the excitement of houses and trees and fields flying past. Thankfully she was asleep by the time we got on the boat and when she woke, the coast of Ireland was in sight.

When we walked into the kitchen in Carlow you could have knocked the ma and da down with a feather. My sister, Phil, was at the open oven basting the roast beef.

'In God's name why didn't you let us know?' said the ma.

'You're a proper bastard, Danno', said the da, 'thinking you can turn up when you like'.

'So, this is Fern. Give us a look at you', Phil was all over her. 'Why didn't you bring your mammy?'

The brat's lips got all quivery and I knew we were going to be treated to a bit of sobbing. You could see Phil had taken to her.

'C'mon, Fern, would you like to see a little puppy dog?' says she and off they went hand in hand.

I told the ma and da that Rosie had left me and taken to the streets. That I didn't know she was a whore when we got married. In the end they offered to keep the young one until I would be free to bring her back to London.

When I left that evening, I didn't say goodbye or anything. The brat was playing with the puppy. That's the way I remember her. Amazingly Rosie never tracked me down. There was nothing in the papers. For a while I was a bit jumpy when there was a knock at the door or I'd see a policeman.

When Phil married the louser she was going out with, the brat went to live with them. In recent years I'd send her the odd Christmas card with a few quid, but there's never a thank you, never a card back.

Translated by the author

The Couch Potato

He was as usual sprawled on the couch in the front room watching a John Wayne video at full volume. Although he found any movie on the small television screen riveting enough, you could safely say that John Wayne was his specialised subject. For the past two hours he had been engrossed in *Tall in the Saddle*. Now he had switched to *Red River* and was driving one of the great cattle herds of the world along the Chisolm Trail yet another time.

She herself must have seen that video half a dozen times. That was in the early stages of his addiction when she was trying to do something about their relationship without realising it was already in terminal decline. These days she couldn't stay in the same room with him anymore. It was so irritating the way he said the lines bang on cue along with John Wayne. It really got under her skin.

Now the cattle were stampeding, heading in a cloud of dust for the canyon. The house shook as they thundered down the hall and into the kitchen where she nursed a cup of coffee and listened to 'Dook' Gleeson whooping and hollering from his couch along with the best of them. Yahoo! Yahoo! Giddyup! A million violins were going mad in the background. She wondered how long more her nerves could stand it.

He hadn't always been 'Dook'. When she'd known him first, as a schoolgirl, he'd been Tommy Gleeson, one of Mammy's lodgers. Then when Mammy was whisked off to hospital with peritonitis in the middle of the night and died before morning, the other lodger moved out but Tommy stayed.

At the time she was grateful not to have been left on her own. She was twenty and shocked and frightened by Mammy's death. An only child, she had never found it easy to make friends. She remembered her father vaguely. He had gone off to England the summer she was six and simply never came back. Mammy never talked about it. She got on with running the boarding house and tried to make the best of life. Not in a martyrish way, of course, but it couldn't have been easy on her, what with the neighbours whispering and a small child to rear. After her death, Tommy, in some strange way she couldn't explain, was a link with her. He seemed to be solid and sensible and advised her to let two more rooms in order to supplement what small money she was to inherit. He was kind in those days.

Chrissie, Mammy's friend from number 24, thought otherwise. She dropped in the morning after the funeral.

'Sit down, Pauline'. She said looking uncomfortable. 'We've got to talk. Look, give yer man his notice. He's taking advantage of you'.

'He's ok, Chrissie. He's no bother really'.

'Get rid of him, pet. He should know better'.

'What do you mean?'

Chrissie's eyes flickered away from hers.

'He's ten years older than you ... and, well he should know better'.

'He pays his rent'.

'You go train for something, Pauline. Get yourself a job.

But she didn't. That is, not for a while. And he stayed. She sort of drifted from week to week and from month to month, eventually drifting into his bed. Looking back, she couldn't remember quite how it happened. She was one of the spineless jellyfish the nuns warned about at school. No spunk. No backbone. She drifted with the tide.

All right, so it wasn't passion. It wasn't love. She was lonely, looking for friendship, for someone to cushion her against the world. At first it seemed to her that he did that. Besides, Mammy had liked him. She said he was a decent sort. He was a counter-hand in Fitz's hardware shop. Training for management, he said. They married.

It was quieter in the front room now. He must be out in hot dry country urging along the exhausted cowpokes. The buzzards would be soaring overhead. Soon they would pitch camp, their fires glowing in the dark, the coyotes closing in and the cattle getting so nervous a sneezing nighthawk might set them off. Tommy would be feeling that little hunger worm gnawing away at his stomach as he watched the bacon being fried over the campfires. She put a couple of rashers and sausages and some thick slices of black pudding on the pan.

'Dook, how are you!' she muttered sourly as she stabbed the sausages with a fork causing them to retaliate and spit their hot juices at her.

Some of the customers in Fitz's thought he looked like John Wayne. They were the first to call him by Wayne's nickname, 'Dook', and give him notions. God knows they had a lot to answer for. If they could see him these days. He was nothing short of pathetic with his Texan drawl and woman-hating eyes. And he was such a bore going on and on about markets for beef in Missouri in the eighteen sixties without as much as a clue what a bit of sirloin steak for his dinner would set her back.

He'd lost his job three years ago when Fitz's rationalised and became a supermarket. Fortunately by then she was working as a receptionist with Doctor Brady. Chrissie had managed to persuade her to do a secretarial course in the Tech. That was the makings of her. She began to smarten up, take a bit of trouble with her appearance, go out the odd night to the pub with her newly-made friends from the class.

Tommy just switched off and took to the couch, solacing himself with life on the ranch, plenty of target practice and keeping the Comanches at bay. He had no intention of ever doing another day's work. He wasn't interested in her comings and goings. If she complained at all of being tired at the end of the day, or of him not pulling his weight, 'Dook' Gleeson was outraged.

'Will you quit bellyaching, woman', he'd shout. 'I never feel sorry for anything that happens a woman'.

Lines straight from John Wayne's mouth. It was serious when he couldn't find words of his own to converse with her. Maybe she should confide in Doctor Brady. But then she reasoned, Tommy was basically harmless. A bit like the loads of men who dressed up in women's clothes and wore make-up in the privacy of their homes or lived out their *Playboy* fantasies behind closed doors. Being John Wayne was, well, more or less the same, except for the level of the noise.

Chrissie told her that she was a fool to put up with his behaviour, but let's face it she'd always had a set against him.

'You could have that fellow committed in the morning!' she said.

'Committed!'

'Sure. Can't you see he's a few sandwiches short of a picnic?'

'That's a bit over the top. He's just gone a little odd. Losing the job and all'.

She knew she wasn't even convincing herself.

'You call living on a Hollywood set day in and day out a little odd? Cop yourself on, girl'.

She wished Chrissie would shut up.

'I've a lot to be grateful for', she said quietly.

'Like what?'

'Well, suppose he wore a stetson and spurs and went hollering and lassooing and shooting around town?'

'They'd put him in a padded cell and you could get a life'.

She cracked an egg on the pan, careful lest she break the yolk. He was particular about things like that. She cut two thick slices of soda bread and dipped them in the bacon fat. He loved his fried bread. Still, there must be something she could do. She wasn't thirty yet and there was no way she was going to spend the rest of her life waiting on 'Dook' Gleeson, watching him sprawled on that couch, going zap, zap, zap into the next millenium. And if he thought that she was going to feel guilty about not being able to bear babies he had another thought coming. Those days were over. She had suffered enough with three miscarriages.

She took his tea on a tray up to the front room where the curtains were drawn against the summer evening light. Latimer had just died under the hooves of the stampeding cattle. Tommy was glued to the screen.

'Shhhhh'. He said even though she hadn't as much as opened her mouth. He felt he had a God-given right not to be interrupted.

She liked Latimer. He was the one who rode a cute little buckskin mare and wanted to buy his wife a pair of red shoes when he got his pay. Now he was dead and his wife would never get the red shoes.

She placed the tray on Tommy's stomach. He eased himself into a half-sitting position and began to wolf down his fry. She reached for the control and pressed the pause button. The picture froze. His eyes never moved from the screen.

'Me and Chrissie are going over to the cemetery to do up Mammy's grave'.

He jerked a little, sloshing some tea onto the tray.

'To-morrow's cemetery Sunday', she said by way of explanation.

He said nothing. She pressed the pause button again setting the film running and looking back from the door she saw the blueish light from the screen pick out the little globules of grease on his chin.

There was a good crowd in the cemetery clipping and raking and weeding. Some of the old graves had been neglected from this time last year as the dead had no living relations. She thought that was very sad. She checked up on Mammy's grave every month and not one single time had Tommy gone with her. She was glad to have Chrissie tonight.

'Poor Mammy', she said looking at the headstone. 'She'd no life. I mean to die at forty two'.

'She enjoyed herself in her own way. Look at yourself hitched to that no-good and you so young'.

'It mightn't be for much longer, Chrissie'.

She was trying to mix some cream-coloured roses with pink carnations. She didn't have much feeling for flower arrangement.

'Here, let me do that', said Chrissie. 'There's something I've wanted to tell you for a long time and maybe it'll help you make up your mind'.

She felt suddenly threatened and frightened by Chrissie's tone. Her breath was coming in little nervous pants.

'Don't', she said, 'please don't'.

Chrissie went on as if she hadn't heard.

'Your Mammy didn't die of peritonitus. She was pregnant. Six months'.

'No, no, you must be wrong. You've got it wrong'. She was gabbling.

Chrissie paused, fingering the last creamy rose.

'The baby was stillborn. Your Mammy died on the delivery table. One of those embolism things'.

She shivered in spite of the warm August evening. Chrissie got up and put her arms around her.

'There's more', she said slowly. 'She was having it off with Tommy'.

Her body went rigid with cold icy rage at how he had duped her. She pushed Chrissie from her. She'd go home and murder him! She'd strangle him with her bare hands!

'Hey, don't get mad, love. Get even', Chrissie said.

On Tuesday, when 'Dook' Gleeson came back from collecting the dole, he had four videos in a plastic bag. She watched from behind the lace curtains as he opened the front gate, walked up the small garden path and tried his key in the lock over and over again. She smiled, imagining his bafflement. She felt much calmer now, confident that her plan would work out. She had nearly blacked out at the cemetery Mass on Sunday thinking of Mammy and the baby. And then Tommy and herself. It was stomach-turning. Hardest of all was not letting on to Tommy what she knew.

He was going around by the back door now. The locksmith had changed the locks in record time when he was out. The windows were securely fastened. She heard his steps coming round by the front again. Now he was shouting through the letter-box.

'Let me in! Damn you! Let me in!'

She heard the crash of glass as he hurled the little stone bird-bath through the front room window. A second later she saw the squad car pull up and the police bundling 'Dook' Gleeson into the back seat.

After lunch, there was just the formality of signing the commitment papers. Doctor Brady assured her she had more than enough evidence. He'd get the best of care in St Dympna's.

Translated by the author

WIVES

'You were a person I esteemed. I thought you were exemplary in every way and now it is clear to me that you are the lowest form of human life', Tom scowled at me, the corner of his mouth arching with distaste.

A cloud went over my sun. Things had somehow gone seriously wrong. In one way, I didn't want to know anything, but the reverse was how would I ever rest without knowing? I thought I would die there and then. The weight of Tom's contempt floored me. Just what had he found out? I had been so careful. I thought it best to stay quiet, play for time and hear what else he had to say. Besides he sounded so bumptious coming over all judgmental like that and there was something disquieting about the way he didn't question me. Surely I merited an explanation.

We were in the kitchen which looked out on the back garden under a poultice of sycamore leaves. It had been raining all morning so the children were housebound. The three younger ones made a racket in the playroom next door. Kate, the eldest, was practising the tin whistle in her room. I could hear the galloping notes of *Saddle the Pony* repeated over and over again. She was coming on.

Tom and I had our differences but we were able to discuss problems and reach a solution. He was completely dependent on me and knew it. What other woman would he find to take over the running of his house and treat his four children as her own?

Well, of course, it suited me. In the beginning it was part of teaching Denis a lesson. I had been going out with him for seven years and every year we were going to be married the next year when he didn't have to mind his ailing mother. Suddenly I felt betrayed. I was twenty-five years old and had quite enough of waiting for Denis.

'I've landed myself a job in Galway', I told him. 'I'll be starting next week'.

This wasn't the truth exactly as nothing was settled between Tom Ryan and me.

'You can't', he spluttered, 'I mean, Minnie, what about us?'

'Yeah. What about us? You tell me. Where are we going?'

He looked stunned. 'You're so impatient, if you'll only wait we'll work things out', he muttered.

'Phone when you're ready and we'll settle the wedding date'.

Tom interviewed me in the Warwick Hotel in Salthill. I watched him come in, look around the foyer for a minute and walk in my direction. He was a fine cut of a man. Tall with a confident walk, he was sure of his charm. I liked that. Denis's dithering had me cheesed off.

'Are you Minnie Foley?' he smiled.

He would have been about forty years of age and had the sort of flirty eyes of a man who enjoys the company of women. He put me at my ease straightaway asking after my journey and ordering coffee. I noticed that he ordered coffee for three.

'You're younger than I imagined', he said, looking at a woman heading in our direction. 'Ah, here's my sister Maura at last. She's been helping me out with the kids'.

It was clear that she was the one who was checking out my suitability.

'You realise that Cormac is only one year old. How do you think you'll cope?' she asked pleasantly.

I told her that I had started training as a children's nurse but had to give it up when my father died, leaving my mother dependent on me for help with the children at home. I said that as the eldest of seven I was well used to babies. She listened closely to everything I had to say. I liked them both, but said I wanted to meet the children and see the house before committing myself. That seemed to impress them.

It was a large house that Tom had inherited from his parents, comfortable enough but every place cried out for a coat of paint. The room suggested for me was actually a self-contained granny flat with a tiny kitchen, sitting room and bedroom *en suite* which had been their mother's in old age.

Maura stayed for a week to show me the ropes and I was grateful for that but she had to return to Manchester where she was a hospital matron. From her I learned that Cormac was the child of Tom's second marriage; that poor Maeve had died of cancer when the child was eight month's old. The three older children belonged to his first marriage to Claire who had died at Jane's birth.

'I know what you're thinking', Maura said. 'He was fast off the mark getting married so quickly again. He was. But what could the poor man do? He had to be practical. Apart from that Claire and Maeve were great friends. She was always around the place so it seemed the most natural thing in the world that Tom would marry her'.

'I suppose they were in love'.

She shut her mouth firmly. She had said too much.

After she left it was difficult for us all. I realised that things would go against me from time to time but I was confident that I would succeed and that's what happened. The baby became my baby. It was easy to pretend he was my own. The youngest girl, Jane, being four, took to me after a few months. It was harder on Kate and Bobby as they were fond of their stepmother. Not that they gave me any trouble, the opposite in fact. Indeed I thought they were a little too quiet. By degrees I tried talking to them.

'I'd never try to take the place of your mother or stepmother. I'm your friend', I reassured them.

'Are you married, Minnie?' asked Kate.

I burst out laughing. 'I'm not. But I might be before long'.

'Who to?'

'To Denis'. Suddenly memories intruded like a cold wind under the door that grew and gathered in a storm of loneliness around me. In God's name what was I doing in this house so far away from him?

'You're crying', said Bobby.

'No. I'm just lonely'.

'If you marry, you'll have to leave us', said Kate.

'I'll be here for a year at least'.

'Our daddy has got loads of girlfriends', Bobby boasted.

'Where did you hear that?'

'Mrs Burke. Well she didn't tell us, but she was whispering to her friend', interrupted Kate.

'She said he was a phil ... phil ... something', said Bobby.

'A philanderer', said Kate.

'And what is a philanderer?'

'Do you mean to say you don't know? I found out in the dictionary'.

She repeated the word dramatically, lingering on every syllable.

'Such a very long word and you understand it'.

'Yes', they answered solemnly.

The children and I were thrown very much together as their father was away frequently on business. I can't remember when exactly I began to get curious about Tom except that his past held a fascination for me.

Certainly everything changed on my side after I was a year in Tom's employment. Denis and I had met every free day I had and he gave the appearance of being loving at those meetings. Then his mother died and I went back for the funeral. We had a heart to heart talk and I had to accept that he had no intention of marrying me when he told me he was off to Australia for a year and I wasn't part of the plan. Worse, he had a new girlfriend, eighteen years old, and she was going to travel with him.

Yes, of course, that must have been when I began to develop the intense curiosity about Tom, his business and relationships. I'm not a nosy person but I found myself poking into every nook and cranny in the house. I rummaged in Tom's chest of drawers knowing it wasn't right. I felt furtive and mean and didn't know what I was looking for except maybe some clue about his past. I did my best to give up this compulsive behaviour but failed. It was like a disease tormenting me. I was consumed by curiosity, jealous of all the other women in his life, both living and dead – especially the living. I took to scouring his car when he returned after a business trip. I was like a hound sniffing for perfume, a rib of hair, anything that would prove that a woman had been in the car with him. From time to time I found evidence – an earring, a pink key-ring, a lipstick, a copy of *Cosmopolitan* – which I locked at the top of my wardrobe.

Yes I suppose I had fallen in love with Tom but I was intruding on his private life in a most unforgiveable way. If anyone had nosed through my life and my belongings in such a way I would have felt angry and violated. However I continued. I read old love letters from Maeve in the desk in his bedroom. I read them so often I knew them by heart and justified what I was doing by telling myself that it was harmless, that I was only building up a picture of the man. Nevertheless I was quite upset to see how happy he looked with both of his wives in old snapshots in the family albums which were strewn around the living room for all to see.

Another year passed and then events changed. There was a knock on my door one night as I was preparing for bed. I thought that one of the children might be unwell. I unlocked the door and saw Tom.

'Minnie', he said, 'I'm lonely tonight. Come on down and we'll have a drink and a chat'.

It was obvious that he had had a bit to drink already, but I put on my dressing gown and went with him. He had hot whiskies ready for us.

'How much sugar?' he asked.

I knew that I had better be careful since I wasn't used to whiskey. But I needn't have worried. Tom talked about the loneliness of his life and explained to me why he didn't have more time for the children. I told him about Denis and he listened carefully to all I had to say.

'Denis is a waster! A lovely girl like you. It's hard to imagine it', he said.

The following week the same thing happened, the knock on the door just as I was going to sleep. This time he hadn't been drinking.

'Minnie, have you a minute? I'm famished with the hunger. I've had nothing to eat all day'.

'I think there's a little chicken left', I said, surprised that he hadn't got it for himself.

'I've a Chinese take-away downstairs. Will you share it with me?'

He lit a candle and turned on soft music. Tom told me how much his life had changed since I came. I was nearly in heaven. Because I was lonely myself I could understand fully his loneliness after his wives' deaths. And so our weekly dates continued for a couple of months until one night he came to my bed. In a way I invited him since I had stopped locking my door. He was in love with me! My love wasn't one-sided, my fantasies foolish and without base! I stopped the searching and snooping. There was no need anymore.

The neighbours accepted me from the first day. They helped me with the children and were a mine of information about Tom. I knew that Mrs Burke gossiped about everyone but I liked her.

'Ah, poor Maeve', she said to me one day, 'she never knew Tom was carrying on with that young one up in Tuam'.

I was amazed. Hadn't I read the love letters? 'He wouldn't', said I. 'I'd find that hard to believe'.

'Believe it or not, sure it's common knowledge. Are you going to let on now that he hasn't made a move on yourself?'

I reddened and laughed heartily. I hadn't a notion of telling her anything.

'A grand girl like you would make a fine wife for him and the children are daft about you', Mrs Burke winked slyly.

'Sure I'm mad about them too'.

'I'm afraid he has other ideas, Minnie', she said quietly.

I thought I saw a pitying look in her eyes. 'What do you mean?'

'I heard he'll be tying the knot again'.

'You're not serious', I felt faint but there was a chance it was only speculation.

'With the one from Tuam?' I enquired.

'No. An older woman, Charlotte, another friend of Claire's'.

Oh my God! With all my foraging and detective work how could this have escaped me? I was so blind. There it was under my nose all the time. That is to say that the clue was on Tom's bedside table. A book on lake and river fishing in Ireland and inscribed, *With love Charlie*. I was finished. What would I do? But wasn't he in love with me? Mrs Burke must be mistaken. I started fine-combing the place again. I was ashamed. I should have had more trust in our love.

'You are the lowest form of human life', he said.

I continued looking out at the garden under its poultice of sycamore leaves. There were rain-puddles gathering on the tarmac. What had started like a game innocently enough had grown beyond my control. Why didn't I tell him about my detective work? Make a funny story of it? I understood now that as with any addiction I needed help.

Tom wasn't through talking yet.

'Your calls have been monitored by the Gardaí … traced to this house. Why on earth did you have to harass Charlotte?'

'I have no idea what you are on about', I said finding my voice.

'The game is up, Minnie. You had better pack your bags and be gone by morning'.

I was in bits. My love talking to me like this! I was caught in a nightmare!

'She didn't do anything. It was me', Kate's voice came from the doorway.

'And me'. Bobby's voice came from behind her.

'You!' Tom gasped. 'For God's sake, why?'

The whole story came out of what was initially a bit of sport. They overheard gossip between Mrs Burke and a friend and understood that I would have to leave if Tom married Charlotte. Then, inspired by a thriller they had watched on television, they began the secret phone calls. They didn't mean to threaten Charlotte but hadn't wanted her as a stepmother.

Tom was angry and mortified. He wasn't able to meet my eyes. I was saved. There was no need for me now to confess my snooping into his private life but I was extremely hurt and stood firm on one point – that I receive a letter of apology from Charlotte for blaming me in the wrong.

'Now, children, I would like to speak to your Dad privately', I said, and they went.

Suddenly I felt that Tom was nervous in my presence, that I had the upper hand.

'Why didn't you tell me about Charlotte? You pretended that you were in love with me. And you engaged to her! I suppose you are in love with her too and with the girl from Tuam!'

He said nothing.

'A few minutes ago you were trying to get rid of me … ordering me to pack my bags. Well I can't. I need help'.

'Help?' he said dourly.

'I'm pregnant, Tom. Our babies will be born before Christmas'.

'Babies? Christ! Twins?'

'No, Tom. We have three'.

He was quiet for a moment. Then he burst out laughing and put his arms around me. In the end we were both in fits of laughter. I suppose I was agitated but ultimately I had to be sensible and get an explanation. I didn't take in much except that he was going to stick by me and that Charlotte had never understood him. The same old story! I forgave him. Well, I didn't have much choice. Does a woman ever understand a man?

Tom had a friend who was a Garda Detective Sergeant and he had the matter hushed up. He recommended that Kate and Bobby should see a professional counsellor who would help them deal with their problems. Tom spoke to Charlotte. I never heard what passed between them other than she had taken up a post in Cork. The following month Tom and I were married in Rome. Maura came from Manchester to look after the children.

They say that a leopard doesn't change his spots but I think that Tom has learned a lesson. I keep a sharp eye on him and Mrs Burke is on my side, keeping an ear cocked for any rumours. The triplets aren't born yet and Tom stays at home every night to take care of me. My prying days are not over – you will understand. I know well that they never will be, but I don't feel guilty anymore.

Translated by the author

THE DICEMAN

It started with a roll of the dice. Not any old roll or any old dice. It came right out of the blue, or should I say the intense singing blue of a North Dakota summer sky. Momentarily I didn't believe it. I really thought I'd flipped it this time. I lack confidence in myself, you see. But it was no illusion. There it was spinning to a halt on the warm pavement exactly under the wheels of my child's buggy. I stood like a hypnotised rabbit choking back my fear, staring at it. I was strangling. Six emerald-green pips shining at me defiantly from a beige background. A child's dice from a child's board game. It could only be Melvin with a rotten sick joke.

But where was he? I looked around desperately. Did he throw it from a passing car? Was he lurking behind a tree or a fence tossing it towards me with deadly accuracy? How on earth did he find me out? Ok. I might as well face facts, the sonovabitch had tracked me down or else his private eye had. A six too. He knew how to throw sixes. Had it brought down to a fine art. I continued to stare at the dice wondering if

I should go to the police, but I knew I wouldn't have a chance in hell. After all I was the one who had run away and deserted the family home. He was so cunning too. He would prove that I was unfit to be a mother and he'd get custody of the child. So I left the dice with its six emerald-green eyes staring at the dazzling sky and hurried home.

That was a mistake because it was exhibit one and when I told my analyst about the incident it was kind of obvious she didn't believe me.

'Cathy', she said, 'let's talk this thing through. Are you quite sure you weren't imagining things?'

Tears of frustration sprang to my eyes. She was my friend, my confidante for the past eighteen months since I'd come to Grand Forks. Now she was distancing herself. Was she in Melvin's pay? He would go to any end to prove my ineptitude and gain custody of the child.

'And the Valium, Cathy? It can leave you a bit foggy you know?'

Oh shit! I'd have to get a new shrink. I'd have to up and move anyway if I was to outwit Melvin.

Almost as if she was reading my mind she said: 'Don't think of running away again, Cathy. Stand your ground. Melvin won't take the child'.

It was all fine and dandy in the beginning. We'd been married in Eureka Springs, Arkansas. It was so romantic, the mountain slopes, the waterfalls, the woods. The perfect place for a honeymoon. Melvin was greatly taken by 'The Holy Land' theme with its Sea of Galilee, the River Jordan and Golgotha, not to talk of the gigantic statue of Christ of the Ozarks, seven storeys high with his arms reaching out for ever. He went on and on about it, not that he was at all religious, but as I was beginning to realise, a bit obsessive. This holy stuff just seemed to grab him. Maybe like the *Snakes and Ladders* game. He didn't come clean on that one for a long time. Melvin can be quite secretive but I should have copped on the S&L thing earlier if I hadn't been so besotted with him. You might say I rushed into marriage before he could change his mind.

We didn't have a whole lot of cash to blow on the honeymoon but it worked out really great. We'd have lunch in the Eureka Egg Emporium at Basin Park on Spring Street. Melvin adored his food. What we saved on the lunch specials we could spend in Joe's Mexican Restaurant on Main Street. You'd die for the red snapper there.

I suppose I never actually minded Melvin fidgeting before. He was one of those guys with restless hands which may have denoted inner tension. Like, he was always fidgeting with his cutlery, with the pepper and salt and sauce bottles, with the coins in his pocket. I thought he tended to fidget with me too. It made me all squirmy and twitchy. I could never get him to handle me the way I wanted. Now, in Joe's place, he kept fiddling with a dice, dropping it on the table between us, lifting it, throwing it again. It was a bit weird but I said nothing. I didn't like to squash the guy. Anyway he seemed to sense my mild irritation.

'Something wrong, sweetheart?' he asked.

'No', I answered quite truthfully.

The dice didn't in all honesty bother me, but let's face it, it was a distraction and it was hard to keep my eyes from following its movement. Hard also to keep my mind on his conversation. Melvin liked my undivided attention.

By the time we got back to LA and into our new home at Redondo Beach, Melvin and me were playing

Snakes and Ladders in bed every night. When I thought about it objectively I couldn't believe how easily I had fallen in with his wacky recreation. I was never remotely interested in board games. They were so old fashioned. But there I was throwing stupid dice night after night. How the hell was I to know that S&L were his big turn on and not me? Of course winning was essential to his excitement. That is why he usually managed to fiddle sixes. Well maybe I'm not being fair but I reckoned it was some form of cheating that I couldn't spot or why did sixes turn up for him so often and for me not at all? My analyst explained his problem to me but it didn't help much. She thought he was stuck in some youthful time warp when he may have had some intense sexual pleasure while playing S&L so the game became a sort of fetish with him. The whole thing was weird but I always said, so long as we were happy. But then were we happy? Melvin sure was.

We tried for a baby for four years but nothing was happening so I had all the tests done and came out with flying colours. It was Melvin's turn. He wasn't too keen. I swear he was absolutely contented to go on with his damn board game. I mean he was so stuck in his ways.

'Hey, Mel', I wheedled him in bed at an opportune time. 'I'm getting kinda bored with Snakes and things'.

'Then you got yourself one helluva problem, sweetheart', he said.

I didn't like his tone. It was intense and threatening. I didn't like his face either with his sandy eyebrows meeting furiously in the middle. His reaction was a bit over the top.

'There are some great computer games', I burbled.

'Give us a break'. He scowled and turned his back to me.

I almost cried but I wouldn't give him the satisfaction. It suddenly struck me I wasn't sure if I even liked him anymore.

Melvin was definitely changing. He had something on his mind and it wasn't work. He finally confessed that he'd been to the clinic and the diagnosis was that he had a low sperm count.

'That's no big deal, honey', I told him.

'It's the worst thing that could happen to me. I'll never have a son'.

'Hey, hon, don't worry. It's a world trend in men'. I tried to reassure him. 'We'll just have to try harder'.

Melvin doesn't give up easily. I'll say that for him. He went shopping and came back with all sorts of books on his problem plus an enormous white cotton nightshirt. I wondered if he was going to take off to the desert. But no. He donned this garment every evening after work. It became his uniform at weekends. He mowed the grass in it, went shopping in it, wore it drinking carrot juice under the jacaranda tree. I thought he looked a trifle eccentric but he said that the shirt was ideal for his condition as he had been advised by his doctor not to wear anything constrictive. This apparently applied to his ponytail which he released as well from its customary binding.

The scheme worked because within six months I was pregnant with twins. Melvin who had a sort of soap opera mentality then became obsessed with having a son and heir.

'For Chrissake! Heir to what?' I questioned.

'God, you're so literal', he said. 'Every man wants a son to play baseball with. To go fishing with'.

'Bullshit! You don't play baseball. You don't fish'.

I was so cheesed off I could have hit him.

The twins were born and Melvin got his son alright but he was stillborn. He mourned him and wept for him and it broke my heart to watch them. Suddenly I knew with horrible clarity that he would be trying for a son again. Years of *Snakes and Ladders* stretched ahead of me, the empty thud of the dice, the huge white nightshirt. I had to escape fast.

The chance presented itself when Melvin went back to Arkansas to bury our son in a small cemetery within sight of Christ of the Ozarks. While he was gone I packed a few belongings and vanished with our daughter without trace. Or so I thought.

My analyst was right about one thing. I'd have to stop running. A few days passed and Melvin made no further dramatic gesture. Still, the damn dice with the emerald-green pips lay engraved in my mind. Then on the third night as I was pulling the drapes, I noticed I was being watched from a car opposite. I didn't think it was Melvin but I could check. I dialled our number in Redondo Beach. It was my own voice on the answering machine. I put the receiver down, none the wiser.

A noise woke me sometime during the airless night. I leapt out of bed and checked the baby's cot. She was sound asleep but in the dim glow of the night-light I saw the dice on the coverlet, its green pips staring at me. Fearful lest I frighten the child, I stifled my scream and searched the apartment thoroughly but Melvin had gone.

By morning I was exhausted with lack of sleep and went into the bathroom to shower. I had to step over his damp towels on the floor. The smell of his shower gel was overpowering. I went back to the cot, brought the child into the bathroom and locked the door.

After breakfast I tried the Redondo Beach number again. Melvin's voice answered. I was baffled. This had to be some sort of trick. I listened and said nothing. Melvin shouted excitedly.

'Cathy, it's you. I know it's you. Come on, sweetheart, tell me where you are'.

I sobbed just the tiniest bit.

'Cathy, say something'.

I couldn't. I clung to the phone listening.

'Ok, you don't have to tell me where you are. Listen, I've been going out of my mind with worry'.

Was he having my call traced? I was getting so confused. He must know my whereabouts if the private eye was reporting back. And what about the bathroom?

Melvin's voice continued nice and rumbly like the sea.

I cracked. 'I'm fine. But stop playing games with me'.

'Are you having me on?'

'Who put the dice in the baby's cot last night right beside her little face?'

'Oh, Cathy! What dice? What baby?'

I screamed at him. 'Your baby daughter, who else?'

'Our babies died, Cathy. You know that'.

I slammed down the phone. You see this is the way he tortures me. I lifted the child gently. It was time for her walk.

THE SECRET

She liked the barn loft. It was a good place to hide.
Especially on days like this when her aunt was so busy
cleaning the parlour and doing the baking. There was
a warm nutty smell from the grain and the different
sacks of meal that lined the walls. Sometimes she
played with the grain in the open sacks, letting it spill
through her fingers, or if she was certain that there
was nobody around the yard, she made pictures with
it on the floor. She could make robins and a sun with
rays that stretched out and out. The hardest thing was
a butterfly. She had to be so careful with the wings to
get the markings right. If she didn't choose bright
yellow Indian meal for the spots they didn't show up
properly. Her aunt used to cook the yellow meal for
the pigs in the huge black pot down in the boiler-
house. It tasted nice too, all fluttery and velvety like
eating butterflies. The roof of the loft was quite high
and sloped. There were saddles, reins and horse
harnesses slung over the rafters which were almost
black. Whenever she looked very high she used to get

all shivery. If she stared hard enough, the darkness began to lunge down, shadowing her like a big bat and she had to cover her ears and crouch on the floor making herself so small that it couldn't see her. When it got tired of the search, she could sense it rise up very slowly and go back to its nest under the roof.

Through the narrow cobwebby window she had a full view not only of the yard and the kitchen door, but of the top field and the tarred road that passed the school, passed the chapel, passed the Famine wall and the laneway to their house. If anybody approached the barn there was plenty of time to hide in one of the unused grain bins with lids. She would huddle there listening to her Aunt Lily, calling her from the back door, 'Annie, Annie, Annie'.

She never answered. But when her aunt had gone inside again, she would open the loft door just a chink and squint into the barn below to make sure that nobody saw. Then very quietly she would descend the loft stairs, so silently that the hens didn't even notice her. Not like when her brother Henry came into the barn with his pitchfork to get hay for the byre and the hens kicked up such a hullabaloo with their cackling and scattering before boots.

Nobody would call her today, not with all that polishing going on. The brasses would be shining like toffee and the parlour furniture all proud and twinkling. She made herself comfortable on a pile of jute sacks beside her lookout and scanned the avenue to the house. Her aunt always said 'avenue'. It sounded nice. Today it was raining and the laurels that edged the avenue were flat and shining. Little rivulets of mud carved wormlike channels through the scant gravel and ran until they got trapped in puddles along the way. Henry had cut the grass in front of the house late yesterday when it was dry. He clipped a straight edge around the flower border. The peony roses were spilling over the place, their heads heavy with rain. She liked the garden. Henry did the finishing touches. Aunt Lily said that Henry had taste. Soon the children would be coming out of school. She would watch them hurry home in all directions anxious to be out of the rain.

She wondered what school was like. Henry and Francis played 'school' with her long ago but she tired of it quickly when they got cross with her because she couldn't learn her sums. She preferred helping her aunt make pastry people with raisin eyes. Aunt Lily baked them in the hot black oven and took them out just when they were the right golden colour. She began to feel chilled, then rose, smoothed out one of the sacks and climbed inside, carefully securing it under her oxters. Then she lay down by the window to wait.

Sarah Rafferty was just six months teaching in her first job. She was finding her way by degrees, getting to know people and settling down quite well in the parish school. Obviously it was a change from her training college in Dublin when she felt that she was at the very hub of life. Even if she never went out, there was this feeling of excitement, of people charging around doing important things. It was also very different from the small east coast town where she had grown up with her three sisters.

The country took getting used to, especially the hushed evenings. The fellows were different too. The Dublin lads were simple enough in their own way. You knew where you stood with them. In the country you wouldn't know what they'd be thinking. She was aware that she was under scrutiny all the time. Quiet eyes were sizing her up. Or maybe her mother had made her suspicious

'You do realise, Sarah', she would say, 'that when you take a job in a country place like Belderrig you'll be considered a catch and a good catch at that'.

'Ah Mother', Sarah would groan, 'how would any farmer consider me a catch when I know nothing about farming and I can't as much as boil the proverbial egg!'

But her mother continued, 'You know you can be very naïve, Sarah. Think of the income. Wouldn't it put any farmer on his feet to have a wife who could keep up her job after marriage?'

Her mother thought in terms of economics, having had to cope on her own and educate four children after her husband died. Sarah had a mental picture of herself down on the farm with animals grunting all around her and mud from big boots pounded into every floor. She dismissed the image like a bad thought not to be entertained. Anyway this talk of marriage was a bit unnecessary when she had no intention of settling down for years. Besides she mightn't stay in the country. She felt attracted to getting a position in a good-sized town or even return to home ground. Again the latter might prove unwise as Mother was still somewhat overprotective. In the meantime she loved her work and was anxious to prove that she was a good teacher. She spent hours preparing classes, enjoyed endless walks around country lanes, never returning without wild flowers and grasses for her room. It was a luxury to have a room all to herself in O'Hagan's house which was adjacent to the school. Both at college and at home, she had no choice but to share. Mrs O'Hagan was great company but not in a gossipy way. She filled Sarah in on the background of all the neighbours. She knew that it would help in her work as a teacher. Consequently Sarah felt that she had known some of the more colourful families for years and occasionally had to pull herself up when she realised how slight her acquaintance with them was.

It was on one of her walks that she met two young men at the end of a muddy laneway. They were readjusting a spikey contraption at the rear of their tractor and seemed so absorbed in their work that she would have passed by quietly without speaking. She was studying the opposite ditch when one of them called out.

'Hello, Miss Rafferty, nice evening'.

'Yes, isn't it grand', she smiled.

'I'm Francis Keogh', said the young man, 'and this here is my brother Henry. You are the new teacher aren't you? I don't know how we didn't meet you before'.

She looked at Francis Keogh and liked him instantly. He had a good-humoured face and radiated friendship. Henry had just nodded pleasantly in her direction and continued with his work. He was probably a few years older than his brother and wore an air of responsibility.

'Will we be seeing you at the social on Saturday night?' Francis asked.

'Well, I might be going home. I go most weekends'.

Henry suddenly straightened himself and spoke for the first time.

'Give it a skip this weekend. This is the best night of the year. You'll enjoy it enormously and you'll meet everyone for miles'.

'You are very persuasive', she said, as she fiddled with the flowers in her hand.

This was the beginning. At first they were a threesome going off to a hop or a house-party within a few miles of Belderrig. Bit by bit she found herself falling in love with Henry and he didn't even seem to notice until one Saturday Francis tore a ligament in his leg and stayed at home. Yes, that was definitely the turning point with Henry. Yet he made it so hard for her. She practically had to spell it out for him that she liked Francis as a friend, but that with him – well it was different.

The days passed and brought the end of the school year with the long summer months stretching ahead of her. Sarah knew clearly that she didn't want to leave. So far she had never been invited near the Keogh's house and she could only speculate on what lay at the top of the muddy laneway. Neither had she met Aunt Lily, their father's sister who had looked after the family ever since he had walked out on them a mere four years after his wife's death. Now that was to be rectified this very day when Henry would call at five o'clock and bring her for tea.

Henry had no doubt but that Sarah Rafferty was the woman he wanted to share his life with. She was cheerful and pretty with masses of auburn hair scooped back from her face. It helped also that Francis liked her so much because if he asked her to marry him, Francis would be sharing the house with them for God knows how long. The teaching bit was handy too. He wondered would this be a good time to pop the question? Naturally he hadn't told her much about the family. He was afraid of losing her. Somehow or other an evasive reply came to his lips in response to her questioning. He often thought that she was sifting his answers as if looking for a specific reply. He had a sense of failing her by not being open with her. Not that she persisted with any line of questioning. When she saw his reticence she would switch to talk of school or tell him some funny story she had heard from Mrs O'Hagan. Maybe it was all very innocent, but he felt that she was testing him at times.

He liked being seen with her too. She dressed in browns and greens that flattered her colouring. He was sure that Aunt Lily would agree with his choice. She constantly reminded Francis and himself that she would have to approve of any girl that came in on her floor. When he told her that he would like her to meet Sarah Rafferty she was more than interested.

'Well well, Henry, the little school mistress. Mind you I had heard rumours. Aunt Lily keeps her ears to the ground. I hope you were sensible and didn't mention Annie'.

'I told her nothing and I hate myself for the deception'.

'Get a grip on yourself, boy. You can tell her when you are married. If you do otherwise you'll spoil you chances. A girl like Sarah Rafferty mightn't like to be associated with a family that has someone like Annie'.

Henry was not reassured. 'Everyone remembers we have a sister even though they never see her. They don't ask about her anymore because they'll get no information. I'm sure that Minnie O'Hagan has told Sarah about her and I feel a bit foolish saying nothing'.

Henry fell silent. Aunt Lily must be doting if she really believed that he could propose to a girl and keep the cupboard locked on the family skeletons. He loved Sarah. Why then had he let himself be influenced by Aunt Lily's fears? Francis too agreed with him that he must come clean with Sarah. But how could he look her in the eye and tell her everything? Aunt Lily was right. He would lose her. One way or the other, he had no right to ask any woman to be his wife. The clock ticked away quietly. The light in front of the Sacred Heart grew redder and redder with every passing second until he thought either it or his head would explode. He rose quickly from his chair.

Aunt Lily was decisive. 'You must ask Miss Rafferty for tea tomorrow. We'll have cold chicken. The White Wyandotte is ready for the pot. And we'll have tomatoes and little green onions. I'll make a nice Madeira cake with a bit of American frosting. I'm glad now that the parlour is looking so well with the new wallpaper and paint. Don't you worry, Henry. Everything will be just fine'.

Henry got more worried by the hour. By the time he was due to collect Sarah he was tense and jumpy. They approached his home in silence. Sarah tried over and over again to initiate conversation, but could not break through his preoccupation. This was a new Henry. She couldn't have imagined him like this. The laneway was muddy enough to make her glad she had worn her boots. She had expected that he would have come for her in the pony and trap. Henry was clearly nervous. That must be what was wrong with him. She was the one who should have been uptight since she was going to get the once-over from Aunt Lily. Strangely enough she felt more curiosity than anything else.

Annie from her vantage point saw them approach. She leaned forward to get a better look at her brother with a stern face that was as white as the ducks in the far field and a girl with red hair and shiny boots. The girl below seemed to look straight up at her and smile. Annie was so mesmerised she couldn't pull away.

'Look, Henry, there's someone at the barn window watching us'.

Henry didn't look. 'Ah, it's probably one of the hens strayed up to the loft'.

He pushed open the front door and indicated that she go ahead.

'Come and meet Aunt Lily', he muttered.

His aunt was at her most charming. The parlour gleamed with polish and photos of the boys. Francis was his usual pleasant self, insisting that Sarah draw closer to the fire even though it was a June evening. Henry was marginally more relaxed. The table was laid out with the thinnest of china on a white damask cloth. Red jam glowed in a glass dish. Evenly-sliced brown and white soda bread was lined up on two plates. There was a central platter of meat beautifully garnished, a fancy cake with icing, fingers of fruit cake reclining on lace doilies and a couple of gooseberry tarts. Sarah tried not to stare. Oh, God, she thought, I could never compete with such industry and domesticity.

Out loud she said, 'but you went to far too much trouble, Miss Keogh. This is a wonderful spread'.

Aunt Lily smiled graciously and poured tea daintily from a china pot which she replaced on a little stand beside her and cocooned it with a hand-crocheted tea-cosy of the most intricate stitches. The chit chat flowed. Aunt Lily volunteered that she had been a cook in New York in the early thirties and that gave her great training.

'You have no idea how exacting those New York ladies were, Sarah. And the houses were mansions. I had a maid to prepare the vegetables for me and another to wash up. We would have several dinner parties a week. You never saw anything like the entertaining'.

'You must have found it hard to come back', said Sarah.

'Not at all. Give me Ireland any day. But, what about you, Sarah? Do you like Belderrig? How is the teaching going? I hear great reports of you'.

Sarah laughed at the battery of questions and answered as wittily as she could. All the time she was aware that Henry never tried to enter the conversation. Aunt Lily and Francis seemed unaware of his silence. She tried to catch his eye as he sat opposite her. And here was Aunt Lily again questioning.

'Your family Sarah? All sisters? And your mother? Henry tells me she was widowed young'.

Sarah replied that her father had died of lockjaw but that was before there were injections to counteract it. She and her sisters couldn't even remember him. That's why they didn't feel sad about it.

Then she said suddenly, 'Henry, you never told me how your mother died?'

'Goodness!' said Aunt Lily, 'such sadness. Why don't we clear the table and play cards'.

'Mother died in childbirth', said Henry quietly.

'Was it with Francis?' Sarah's voice was almost a whisper.

'Oh no', said Francis. 'I remember her'.

'Do you play cards, Sarah?' interrupted Aunt Lily.

'Well, not really, Miss Keogh'.

'Never mind we'll teach you'.

Aunt Lily got them all to help with clearing the table and within a short time, Sarah was having the rules of rummy explained to her. By the end of the first game even Henry was laughing. The remainder of the visit was light hearted. Then Sarah, seeing that the evening was growing dark against the undrawn curtains, decided not to outstay her welcome with Aunt Lily. She said her thank-yous and goodbyes promising to come again in the autumn.

Outside a fresh wind had blown the rain away and a watery moon lit up the yard and the barn at the far side. Henry slipped his arm through hers and said very casually, 'I'd like you to meet our sister'.

'I thought you would never tell me', she said. 'You see I've known all along. Mrs O'Hagan told me, but I had to hear it from you'.

Henry slowly reached for the hurricane lamp inside the barn door and put a match to the wick. They stood in its morose light. She could see the faint outline of the loft stairs and the ghostly shapes of farm implements leaning away from the light.

'Why do you say nothing, Henry? Are you angry with me for knowing?'

'No, no. It is something else. Something that not even Minnie O'Hagan knows. Good old Aunt Lily saw to it that none of them knew. Our father walked out on us alright. He walked across the yard, up into the loft and hanged himself. Annie was only four years old when she found him swinging from the rafters. Aunt Lily buried his body. She never told us where. My guess is he is under the barn floor here. Now what do you think of me, Sarah?'

He watched her white face sway between him and the night.

Translated by the author

STAYING THIN FOR DADDY

If she were a bird she'd be a swan. She could watch swans forever. They were so mysterious, so noble, so beautiful. Sometimes on damp summer nights she would walk as far as the Wolfe Tone Bridge to where the Corrib rode the incoming tide and the swans converged to feed on the brackish waters. She would lean on the parapet and see the black ribs and spars of rotting boat-hulks lining the banks as far as the Spanish Arch. And such milky hordes of swans. Galaxies of them jubilant in the moonlight, dipping, diving and surfacing with triumphant beaks.

If she watched them long enough and concentrated hard enough her feet took up the rhythm of their paddling. She felt the elation of the tide beneath her and her neck curving and stretching in a long sinuous S. She never wanted it to end but then the ticking would begin somewhere on the edge of her mind keeping time with the Town Clock at St Nicholas's behind O'Brien's Bridge, and like Cinderella she knew her magic would inevitably be scattered. There would be concrete beneath her feet once more and the long walk out to Salthill.

By day, she mostly went down the slipway at Nimmo's Pier where she could get quite close to her swans. They knew her so well they would eat crusts from her hands. Her next door neighbour kept bread-scraps for her as she never had any leftovers herself. She lived on her own since Daddy died and a little food kept her going. Daddy used to say 'See the swans, Hannah. They are such perfect creatures. Not an ounce of superfluous flesh. You never see a fat swan'. That was so true. You'd see dogs with rolls of fat around their shoulders and cats whose bellies swept the ground, but no, you'd never see a fat swan. Daddy had a thing about fat. Fat revolted him.

'Look at the gut of yer man ...', he'd say, pointng out a bather testing the water at the edge of the sea. 'Isn't he an awful sight?'

Mother was fat. Daddy called her a moving mountain. She smelt of garlic and herbs and fresh root ginger and chopped green mint and runny honey and he didn't like it one bit. Her fingers were dyed yellow, not as you might think from nicotine, but from peeling and chopping onions and carrots. Daddy hated Mother's spicy exotic cooking and what he called the vile Middle Eastern pongs that saturated the house. He lived on steamed chicken breasts and white fish and the whites of eggs. The yolks he avoided as they were loaded with cholesterol. He insisted that his diet was both exciting and safe. He planned on outliving Mother.

'I'll see you shoving up the daisies yet, my girl!' He used to chuckle in anticipation. Mother cooked his lonely little meals in neat flat tinfoil parcels and ladled out lavish dollops of her well-seasoned concoctions to Hannah and her sister.

Hannah couldn't quite remember when she began to realise that Mother and he were at war and that food in some baffling way was central to that war. There were just the four of them in the family. Mother and Daddy, Hannah and her sister, Mona, who was fifteen months younger. Daddy said that Hannah meant 'gift from God'. She knew she was easily his favourite. She always made a special effort to please him because he made her feel so unique and important. Mona was different. By the time she reached thirteen she went out of her way to annoy him at every opportunity. She said he was a pain in the butt and that Hannah was a right eejit to run to his every beck and call.

'Can't you see he's using you like a little pawn against Mother?'

'I don't know what you're getting at', Hannah replied.

But, of course she did. She smiled a secret smile. She was the one that Daddy singled out for treats. She was the one who accompanied him to the cinema or on fishing trips or to the races. It was she who went feeding the swans with him. Naturally she loved Mother too. That went without saying. But she felt sorry for Daddy. Mother and Mona had him for laughs and that wasn't fair.

'Look, Hannah, I'll fix you up with Billy's brother', Mona told her. 'God almighty, you're sixteen years old and still mooning over swans with Daddy! What you need is a real man in your life!'

Mona had started going out with fellas when she was fourteen. She wore such a woman of the world air about her that Hannah felt childish and inexperienced by comparison. But she wouldn't have been seen dead with Billy's brother. He had really bad acne and a missing front tooth that he'd lost in a fight over Agnes O'Toole of all people! The very thought of him made Hannah shiver. Let's face it, Daddy was a hard act to follow. He could be very nice. Very charming. He knew how to behave, raising his hat to women, holding doors for Hannah and always walking outside of her on the footpath. And he was an actor. He acted in plays in the Claddagh Hall. The producer, Father Rafferty, said he could have made a living on the professional stage.

The year she finished school, Hannah studied very hard. She wasn't clever and quick like Mona but she wanted Daddy to be proud of her results. However, what with long hours poring over her books, precious little in the line of exercise and Mother's generous helpings, she put on a few extra pounds around the hips. It was scarcely noticeable, but Daddy wasn't deceived. He detected the stretch on her skirts and was very annoyed. He grew silent and withdrawn. At first Hannah didn't know what she had done to displease him. She mentally went back over all their conversations, sifting her words in an effort to make out how she had offended, but for the life of her she couldn't find a single thing. Anxiety numbed her. Then after three days she finally worked up courage to enquire what was wrong.

'You've put on weight, Hannah', he said quietly, but accusingly.

'No … no', she spluttered in panic. 'Well … hardly any'.

She felt so ashamed. She must look dreadfully ugly to him.

He saw how upset she was. 'It's alright, Hannah', he said, 'you'll take it off in no time. You must, you know'.

She heard herself babbling. 'Yes. Yes. Myself and Mona will be swimming every day and ...'

'Good girl', he interrupted, 'you mustn't put on weight or Daddy won't love you any more'.

'Christ Almighty!' was Mona's reaction when Hannah told her. She didn't really want to tell Mona but she needed to talk to someone.

'You shouldn't listen to him, Hannah. He's a complete fruitcake. Billy's brother thinks you look real sexy'. Hannah didn't care what Billy's brother thought. She just wanted Daddy's approval. She simply couldn't bear it if he didn't love her.

Ever after that she was careful not to put on weight. It was easy once she left home and went to work as a secretary in a solicitor's office in Ballinasloe. She decided to live on her own even though sharing a flat would have been less expensive. The important thing was she could starve if she felt like it and there would be nobody to comment on her eating habits.

Mona married Billy when they were both eighteen and after four years moved to Dublin with a clatter of kids. Daddy was glad to see the back of them. Billy's brother lost his acne, got his front tooth crowned and went off to be a Christian Brother. Hannah went home one weekend to find Mother lying on the kitchen floor beside the cooker with a wooden spoon in her hand, and a succulent smell of herbs and beef wafting from the simmering casserole she was preparing. She died of a massive heart attack, so Daddy got his wish to outlive her.

Life was never the same without Mother. Daddy grew listless when the food-war came to such a sudden end. He seemed quite at a loss what to say or to do once he had changed the house to his own liking. Hannah felt that the kitchen was a forlorn, purposeless place without the enormous presence of Mother and the bubbling and spattering from her frolicsome pots and pans. The ghosts of her herbs lingered on, despite the fact that Daddy had the kitchen repainted. Hannah was sad about that. It was a lovely shade of terracotta that Mother had had specially concocted in the big mixing machine at Corbett's paint shop. Now Daddy painted the kitchen white. It was as if he were trying to exorcise Mother's very essence. It took three coats of paint to cover the terracotta. Anyway there was no more gloating about shoving up the daisies. Daddy must have felt he was the next in line himself. He took to brooding on the transience and charade of living. Coming up to bedtime each evening Hannah heard him sighing about another day being nearly o'er, a journey towards the eternal shore. She recognised that most of what he said was a rehash of lines from old plays he had acted in.

Hannah gave up her job in Ballinasloe to look after Daddy, but he died a short year after Mother, leaving her the house. After the funeral Mona drew her aside.

'I'm worried about you, Hannah. You're so skinny'.

'Rubbish. I'm healthy as a trout'.

'You need nourishment, decent food. You're only thirty-five and I swear you look fifty. He's gone, Hannah. You don't have to stay thin for Daddy any more'.

But she did. She tried. She honestly tried to eat more. And the food choked her. She couldn't be disloyal to Daddy. All the more so now that he was dead.

Down at Nimmo's Pier Hannah edged her way along the slipway. She clutched her plastic bagful of crusts tightly. There was a stiff wind blowing and her eyes watered slightly as they skimmed over the water to the lighthouse and back. The swans had spotted her coming. They were sweeping towards her now over the steely grey waters, mysterious, noble, beautiful. Such milky hordes of them, gracile, jubilant in the dull light. She knew their ravenous craws and the raw currents beneath them. The traffic along Grattan Road faded and soon she felt her body taken over by the rhythm of their paddling, the wind singing in their feathers and her own neck dipping, and stretching towards them in a great curving S. She didn't want it to end. Nearer and nearer they came treading water in their enthusiasm to be with her, spreading out the great span of their wings. Suddenly she began to shake with fear. There was something very wrong. They were angry with her. Hissing her off the pier. Too weak to move she found herself staring into the eternal caverns of their wild beaks. For a moment, she raised her frail arms to protect her face before collapsing under the battering of their ferocious wings and the pounding of their strong webbed feet.

The Venus Trap

Most mornings Mrs Alicia Lacumber opened the door of her bedsit in Number 84 Marlfield Road at eight thirty or thereabouts. Cocking her head this way and that like an anxious wren she listened to the sounds of the house and, if all was clear, she shuffled down the two steps from her bedsit onto the landing and scuttled up the next flight of carpetless stairs to the bathroom with her chipped enamel pail brimming with slops. The neighbours, knowing her routine, were careful not to embarrass her and discreetly timed the opening of their doors.

Once, when I had just moved into Number 84, I opened my door, ready to race up to the shared bathroom and took Mrs Lacumber completely by surprise. She was dressed in her washed-out pink dressing-gown, her grey hair tightly rolled onto pink, sponge curlers that were covered with a purple sleeping net to keep them neat. She tried reversing with the pail the minute she saw me, but stopped when some liquid sloshed about her feet. Her discomfiture was acute.

'You go first', I called out. 'I've got loads of time'.

She didn't reply. She watched like a hypnotised rabbit before a marauding cat. She tried to stammer out something but no words would come. I dropped my eyes and retreated until I heard the sharp snap of her door clicking shut.

Late that evening, as I was squatting on the floor sorting out the last of my bits and pieces from their packing paper, there was a brisk knock at my door.

'Who's there?' I shouted not wanting to get up from my cramped position.

'It's me, Mrs Lacumber', a voice twittered from outside. I hauled myself up and side stepping the gewgaws that barred the way I opened the door. I scarcely recognised the woman I'd seen on the landing that morning. Her hair was slightly bouffant. She had done a bit of back-combing on the crown and forgotten to smooth it over so that it looked like scrunched steel-wool. She was wearing a shapeless knitted two-piece in a nondescript beige colour with a mauve chiffon scarf knotted at the neck. Her skirt was very stained. There was hardly a line on her face but I guessed her to be in her early seventies.

'I won't disturb you, dear', she said all charm and social grace. 'I want to say welcome to you. It's so nice to have a young girl next door to me'.

She made no reference to our previous meeting.

'Won't you come in Mrs ... em I didn't quite catch your name'.

'Lacumber', she replied. 'Mrs Alicia Lacumber'.

'Come in Mrs Lacumber', I said. 'I'm in a bit of a mess unpacking and finding room for things but, I was just about to make a cup of tea'.

'Thank you', she replied graciously. 'Maybe some other time. I'm so busy myself right now. You've no idea. I promised my daughter ... Melanie that is, that I would help out to-morrow. Her husband, Brian, is being transferred to Galway, you know. He's got a lovely job. I'm going to miss them, and my grandson very much, very much'.

As she turned to leave, I noticed the filthy tennis shoes and her bunions pushing through the frayed canvas.

Days and indeed weeks used to go by and I wouldn't meet Mrs Lacumber. But I grew used to her movements. The morning trip to the bathroom. The opening and closing of her door as she led her cats to and from the garden. The daily visits to the huxter's shop in the laneway for milk and sundries.

Once, we met in the downstairs hall and she admired my purple jacket.

'I really adore purple', she told me. 'I buy a lot of purple myself, you know, combs and toothbrushes and hairnets. That sort of thing. And I just love purple flowers like violets and lobelia and irises. My husband used to grow irises specially for me. Wasn't that very thoughtful of him? He used to say, "Alicia, you definitely have royal blood in your veins ... the blood of kings". He had read somewhere, I think it was the *Reader's Digest*, that purple was a royal colour and that those who choose to wear it regularly have delusions of grandeur. Don't you think that a very clever observation?'

She rarely gave me a chance to get a word in edgeways but I managed to intervene.

'Well, it's an interesting theory', I said.

'Oh, no', she said. 'It's much more than that. I can actually trace my ancestors back to Charlemagne through King Pippin, which of course explains my fondness for purple'.

She may have had a fondness for purple but it certainly didn't extend to hygiene. The smells that wafted from her bedsit were indescribably vile. I doubt if she ever opened a window. Sometimes I tried to disentangle the layers of smells. The basic stench was cats, and then the slop-bucket and stale cabbage water and burnt milk and unwashed clothes. This fetid heap of malodour liberally dusted with talcum powder may be pleasant in itself but combined with the other stenches was ... well, plain honest to God sick-making. I've no doubt but that she never washed herself. The three other tenants hogged the bathroom for hours but Mrs Lacumber was in and out in three minutes flat.

By degrees, I got to know her cats, Lawrence and Tee Cee, two insolent toms who had the run of the place but mainly stretched themselves like draught excluders along the front window sill. They had the net curtains in tatters which didn't add much to the appearance of the house from the road. Somehow, I knew without being told that Lawrence and Tee Cee shared the bed with Mrs Lacumber. They had that cosy mattressy look about them.

Hurrying past her door to have my bath one Saturday night, I noticed that it was slightly open and I heard Mrs Lacumber's wheedling tones.

'Open your mouth wide, Georgina. Wide, I said. There, that's better. Now, who's a good girl. Wasn't that yummy scrummy? Let's try another little bit. That was dee-licious, wasn't it my pet?'

Who was Georgina, I wondered. I hadn't heard mention of her. My curiosity knew no bounds and then I was immediately ashamed of myself and tried to banish Mrs Lacumber and her menagerie from my mind.

I met her on the stairs on Sunday shortly after midday. Lawrence and Tee Cee caressed her bony ankles. There was no sign of Georgina. I don't know why she had to keep intruding herself into my thoughts.

'I'm going out with my friends to Sunday lunch, dear', Mrs Lacumber informed me. 'I'm bringing out these naughty boys for a breath of fresh air as I won't be back until quite late'.

'I'm going to be here all day', I told her. 'I'd be glad to let the cats out again. You don't have to rush home'.

'You're very kind', she said, 'but they'll be alright. They have their litter upstairs, you know. And, they're so used to me gallivanting. Sometime, dear, you must come and have lunch with my friends too. They are the Professor Burkes ... perhaps you know them? He is a physicist at the University and dear Mildred is a biochemist. Such clever people. And they are very fond of me. So loyal. We generally play cards after lunch or go for a drive down to Wicklow'.

'Lucky you!' I said. 'Enjoy yourself'.

'That's just what I intend doing', she chuckled as she shuffled off.

I wondered if she would change the dreadful tennis shoes in honour of the occasion.

I couldn't imagine anything colder than my first winter in Number 84. Mornings, after the relentless frosts, the ice was thick on the inside of the window panes. My one-barred electric heater made no impact on the glacial room. Still I pennypinched, putting everything I saved from my miserable wages as a typist into paints and brushes and canvasses. I reckoned that if I were to be the great artist I dreamed of being, then cold and a rumbling stomach was a test of my worth.

So I typed and painted and skipped meals and phoned home weekly saying that I was having a wild time. My sister was green with envy. The line fairly vibrated with her grilling me about my new friends, our parties and get- togethers.

'Oh, Laura', she said in her sugariest voice. 'I can't wait until we get a flat. Only think of the two of us sharing a place between us next year'.

I imagined my mother toasting her shins at a roaring log fire and placidly telling the aunts and cousins, 'Laura's having such a ball in Dublin that we don't see her anymore'.

By mid-January, the snow lay three inches deep on the streets. It struck me that I hadn't seen Mrs Lacumber for a few days, or was it more? I'd been a bit bound up in myself. Maybe she was ill. She could be dead in her bedsit. I found it difficult to recall exactly when I had last heard her shuffle on the stairs. As far as I knew, the other neighbours were indifferent to her, other than to pass the time of day.

When I opened the hall door I took my time scraping off the compacted snow from my boots lest my feet should go from under me on the ancient lino between the sodden door-mat and the stairs. The tenant in the ground-floor flat was cooking onions. I pictured a big pan of them with the juices running out and the crispy burnt bits around the edges. The smell filled the hall and accompanied me up the stairs as far as the second landing where it began to thin out. Suddenly, I saw her under the wan light of the naked bulb outside my door. She looked like a freakish rag-doll slung over the handrail.

'You're ill, Mrs Lacumber', I said as I reached to support her.

'Oh, no'. She caught her breath. 'Just a little tummy upset'.

Her face was contorted with pain and beads of sweat stood out on her nose and forehead.

'You need a doctor', I said. 'Let me help you inside and I'll phone from the hall'.

As I fumbled in my pocket for coins, she seemed to grow worse by the second. Her body shrank smaller and smaller in the big armchair and her thin legs flapped distressfully in the awful tennis shoes. I would have to move quickly.

In the few moments while we waited for the ambulance to arrive, I mentioned her daughter.

'I'll phone Melanie', I said. 'She'll want to be with you'.

'No', she gasped feebly. 'Melanie is not to know. I can't have her worried'. Her voice trailed away.

'Whatever you want', I said, 'but what about the Burkes? You must tell somebody'.

I had to bend over her to hear the faint reply.

'They've gone', she said.

'I don't understand', I pressed.

'They're in Tenerife, they've gone ... for a month'.

The effort seemed to exhaust her and she closed her eyes.

I travelled with her in the ambulance to the hospital. I couldn't very well leave her on her own. Just before she was whisked away from me, she opened her tightly-clenched right hand. I saw the small brass door-key and knew what was bothering her.

'Don't worry about the cats', I whispered, taking the key. 'I'll take good care of them. And your other pet too'.

'Georgina', she breathed, 'Georgina'.

'She'll be fine', I promised.

A nurse came then to get details of Mrs Lacumber.

'Are you a relation?' she asked.

I only paused a second.

'I'm her daughter', I replied. 'Melanie Lacumber's the name'.

'Will you spell that?' she said without looking up.

It was ten past eight by the cheap tin clock on the mantelpiece when I let myself into Mrs Lacumber's bedsit. The smell of dirt and poverty was even more revolting at close quarters. Lawrence and Tee Cee were distraught with hunger. They climbed up my legs clawing at my jacket as if they were sharpening their claws to eat me. I opened a tin of food from one of a stack piled up on the draining board. While they were gorging themselves, I called, 'Georgina! Come here, Georgina. Where are you?'

I couldn't see where she had hidden herself.

I opened the window wide hoping to air the place a little. The tattered curtains blew back in my face. It was snowing again. I turned my back to the window and imitated Mrs Lacumber.

'Georgina', I cooed, 'where's my girl?'

It was then I saw her. She was sitting on a rickety bamboo table in the alcove to the left of the fireplace. Her head lolled to one side, quietly watching me. I thought her little red tongue quivered behind the petalled fringe of her teeth. She was surrounded by her requirements. There was one of those plastic atomiser bottles half filled with what I supposed was water. There was a jam-jar with a selection of creepy crawlies I chose not to examine too carefully. Beside this was a fine, almost surgical tweezers and a delicate souvenir spoon with a blue enamel crest that said *Monaco*.

I took the plastic bottle and covered Georgina with a fine spray. I could see that she revived somewhat. She took on a perky look. I went over and closed the window so that she wouldn't catch a chill. Then, I opened the jar and carefully extracting a morsel with the tweezers, placed it on the pretty green leaf of her tongue. I watched the insect disappear.

'Well, aren't you the clever girl!' I said, 'wasn't that yummy scrummy?'

I groped for another titbit and teased her with it.

'Open your mouth wide, Georgina ... come on, wider'.

She gobbled it up. She looked at me hopefully, but, I was afraid to overfeed her.

My mother phoned. Her voice was anxious. How was I faring with all the snow? My father had business in head-office on the following Friday and could give me a lift home. I put her off, saying the first thing that came into my head. I'd be going to a big art exhibition in Cork with a friend.

I couldn't wait to get back to Georgina.

THE FOR SALE NOTICE

I had the taps of the kitchen sink running full blast, hoping to drown out his words. My back turned to him, I stared through the window imagining his concerned face and the hurt in his eyes. At first he tried to jolly me along.

'Come on Sheila. We're both in this together. Don't you think I've been affected too?'

It was different for him. At least he should understand that. I didn't answer him.

'Look, we'll take another week's holiday before the end of the month', he said, 'it would be nice for Matthew before going back to school'.

'I'm not going with you Dan', I replied frozenly. 'I'm staying right here'.

'Isn't it time you snapped out of it?' he said quietly, 'You can't wallow in your misery forever. Besides it's bad for Matthew'.

I could see Matthew at the far end of the garden. He seemed to me to be a perfectly happy five-year-old. He had a big stick in his hand and was poking with immense concentration at something under the hedge. He had always been a self-sufficient child and found plenty to interest him in the scuttling of beetles and ants under every stone he turned. He rarely demanded my attention these days.

It was August and the Scots pines were dark against a cerulean sky. Meadows and wild flowers swayed in a light breeze between the cottage and the foothills of the mountains. The garden was sleepy and golden. I knew that if ever I was going to do the 'snap out of it' thing, it would be here in this cottage with the smell of heather and honeysuckle in every room.

My mother said that I was an incurable romantic.

'Why by all that's wonderful', she said, 'do you and Dan want to buy a worm-eaten dry-rotting cottage in the back of godspeed?'

'Because we've great ideas for it', I argued loftily. 'You just picture it painted fondant pink with hollyhocks around the door. And honey-coloured wood inside and Liscannor flags on the kitchen floor and a dresser of old platters and rose-strewn chintzes all over the place!'

We saw the For Sale notice quite by accident. We had been driving in Wicklow and stopped by a stream that stampeded away from us dashing off under grasses and ferns as if in fear of its life.

'Let's see where the stream is going', I said.

It was an enchanted animal luring us after it. We followed it for miles down the stony side road.

'We'd better try and turn back', said Dan. 'This road is getting narrower and it's almost green. Looks like a dead end to me'.

'We can turn down there'. I said. 'I think I can see the entrance to a house'.

There was the cottage before us with the For Sale notice almost erased by the weather. I knew that the house had been waiting for us. It appeared to be holding its breath wondering if we would choose it. Its windows were boarded up so we couldn't even peep in. A waspish yellow paint was peeling off the door and the carved wooden eaves.

'Let's buy it!' I said impulsively.

'It's very dilapidated and there's also the little question of money', remarked Dan, 'but we can make enquiries'.

I immediately imagined us living there instead of the estate house in Dublin that was all we could afford when we married. Dan could commute to work and it would be so good for Matthew to grow up in the country.

As it turned out, the cottage was going for a song.

'I'm not surprised', said my mother caustically, 'you'll practically have to rebuild the place'.

I suspected that she and my father were a bit peeved that I planned to put so many miles between us. I set their minds at rest. 'It'll be simply ages before we sell out here and move permanently. We'll just use it as a holiday cottage for the time being'.

'I should jolly well hope so', said my mother, 'you realise you won't have a neighbour for miles in that godforsaken bog and Matthew needs the company of other children'.

I was suddenly aware that I was shivering despite the summer heat. The gushing of the taps into the shallow unplugged sink had splashed through my thin blouse.

I felt cold and drenched to the skin. The water was roaring in my ears as if I was drowning. Dan's hand reached from behind me and turned off the taps.

'Let's pack Sheila', he said, 'we'll come back on Friday if that's what you want'.

I turned and faced him. 'Just go', I said in a dull voice. 'I want you to go away and leave me alone'.

I watched his face redden with anger. He struggled not to say anything but turned on his heel and slammed the door. The dried flowers tumbled from where I had propped them on the old pine dresser and fell to the floor with a whispery tissue-paper sound. When I went to the bedroom to change my wet blouse I saw Dan in the garden lifting Matthew high above his head. The child was laughing and still clutching the big stick. Only moments later I heard the Fiesta engine rev up. When I reached the window Matthew was swinging on the wicket gate and waving after the car.

I don't remember lying down or going to sleep but when I woke Matthew was tugging my arm.

'Come and see my little friends', he said.

'Go ahead', I told him woozy with sleep, 'I'll be out after you'.

I put on my sandals slowly and splashed my face with cold water before following him.

'Look', he said, 'aren't they lovely?'

He moved them round with his stick. They were quite large caterpillars. Maybe twenty of them. They had light green stripes on a dark, greenish-brown background.   'Are they baby butterflies?' he asked.

'I don't know', I said, 'we must look up the butterfly book'.

'We'll have to look after them well, won't we?' he said. 'We don't want them to die like our baby'.

Words froze in my mouth. I couldn't speak. I saw the anxiety in his small face. He was worried about himself and I couldn't reassure him.

A week passed and Dan only telephoned once. I scarcely missed him. Matthew's little friends had multiplied alarmingly in the garden. We discovered that they weren't baby butterflies but Antler moths.

We were having lunch when Matthew said, 'I think the moth caterpillars are so hungry that they are eating up the whole hill'.

'Little things like that couldn't possibly eat a hill, Matthew', I said.

'But I see their paths everywhere', he protested. 'They are like cows. They eat the grass'.

We went outside the wicket gate and across the meadows to where the ground began to rise. I couldn't believe my eyes. Great patches of the hill had been grazed bare. The ground in front of us seemed to shift. It was a moving mass of green striped caterpillars. They were crawling in a stream so thick they must have been six inches deep. I felt sick. Nature was all very well in moderation but this writhing, heaving mass was revolting.

'Watch out', warned Matthew. 'You mustn't stand on them. You'll kill them'.

A dreadful stench of rot and decomposition reached us.

'Look!' Matthew called pointing in the ditch.

I teetered across to him. An army of the creatures was crawling over the corpses of their fellows who lay in a fetid layer beneath them.

I suddenly became aware of the sheer quiet around us. It was uncanny for early afternoon when normally the coo of copulating pigeons reverberated with the ebullient song of birds from the shade of the hazel grove.

'Let's get back Matthew', I said anxiously.

That night when I had tucked him up in bed he insisted that I read him more about moths. I tried to distract him.

'Wouldn't you like the story of the Little White Cat instead?'

'No', he said. 'I want the baby moths'.

By the time he was asleep it was getting dark. I took the torch with me and went into the garden. The caterpillars were everywhere, sheltering under hedges and drills for the night. The big well-fed ones had disappeared and were replaced by a smaller variety. I understood from our reading that the big ones went underground to pupate.

I felt very uneasy. There was little I could do except telephone Dan. But if I told him that we had a plague of caterpillars no doubt he would decide I'd gone clean off my rocker.

Preparing for bed I heard the wind beginning to rise and went around the cottage securing windows. The stench from the hill was blowing towards us filling room after room. When I lay down I couldn't sleep. As the gusts of wind rose and fell my body took up their rhythm. I felt six-month-old labour pains start all over again. I clutched my empty stomach and pushed hard on my grief till I slept sometime around dawn. I knew the sky was beginning to lighten because I hadn't drawn the curtains, so was confused when I woke hours later to a greenish half darkness. Matthew was in the bed beside me.

'They're everywhere', he whispered. 'The caterpillars are all over the windows. It's like being in the car-wash'.

I fought down my panic. We couldn't stay here. We had to get away. I buried my pride and phoned Dan.

'Wait until I come', he said.

'No', I almost shouted. 'We're leaving now. We'll meet you along the main road'.

When I went to open the door, I felt the pressure against it, snatching it from my hands, trying to push it open. A river of the creatures wriggled past me into the kitchen. I tried to pull the door after me, but it was useless. Within minutes they had slithered up the walls and settled down in the foliage of the chintzy curtains. They draped themselves over the carved wooden German clock on the mantelpiece and sizzled to death on the hot plates of the cooker.

'We're going to have to walk on them', said Matthew, 'or we'll never get away'.

We waded as far as the wicket-gate, slipping and sliding on their squashy bodies. I turned then wanting to remember the cottage as we'd first seen it with its inscrutable, boarded-up windows. My fairytale cottage was now a nightmare house. I took a last look at the devastated secret garden hidden from the road and took my child's hand. A flock of lapwings flew in formation over us. The sun silvered their under-feathers as they banked, drawing our eyes to them and guiding us to the road.

FORGIVENESS

Dáithí tossed and turned restlessly beside her. He must have known that she was getting little or no sleep, but still had begged her to stay when she suggested she move to the spare room. She felt his terror, his panic, lest he die alone.

She lay on her back studying the tracery of dark watermarks that webbed the ceiling from the time the roof leaked. She could hear crows take a morning walk across the slates after their bath in the gutters that brimmed from another night's rain. She turned towards him. His face was yellow and he was making a noise in his throat that she hadn't heard before. The stroke that had laid him low three months previously had left his right arm and half his face paralysed. It had changed their lives.

There they were cracking jokes and celebrating his fifty-sixth birthday in Ishbelia, the new Lebanese restaurant. With his usual bravado he was biting into a hot chilli from a salad-bowl in the centre of the table when she saw his face collapse. At first she thought he was clowning, but within seconds she realised that his speech was not pepper induced and his mouth was pulled down to one side. She screamed and a waiter rushed over with a siphon of soda water thinking the hot chilli had distressed her.

'No, no, not me', she shouted. 'Quick, quick, get an ambulance'. She didn't remember much more until it arrived.

She wondered if she would have panicked had it happened at home. What if she had been out? Mowing the lawn for a half an hour? Even talking on the telephone? It didn't bear thinking about.

He was very reliant on her. She had managed to negotiate six months off from Lanigan's, the legal office where she worked as a secretary. She hoped that time and therapy would help. It was a pity that their children were so far away since she had been told family support was vital for his recovery. Seán was in Australia with a wife and young family, while Muireann had settled in New York. Despite friends to whom she could talk, she felt very much alone.

She and Dáithí had a good marriage. She reckoned he was her best friend. Naturally they didn't share everything. He was golf mad. She hadn't the remotest interest in the game. But that was the way it was, something she had to accept with his job in banking. He made valuable business contacts on the golf course and in the sociability of the clubhouse. He was a good provider and as he himself had pointed out, that was his way of showing how much he loved them all.

He was awake when she brought him his breakfast. Coffee, orange juice, yoghurt and a slice of toast with a low-fat spread. Dáithí needed to lose weight and reduce his cholesterol. She knew he was hungry but the diet was worth it if it kept him alive.

'Lucy', he said in his new forced voice that struggled with speech, 'what did I do to deserve you?'

She propped up his pillows and guided him into a sitting position. At least he could help her a little, which was progress. He breathed in the smell of the coffee greedily.

'Is your throat alright?', she asked. 'You were making a funny sound'.

'It's fine. I hate being all this trouble to you'.

'Don't be talking like that! Wouldn't you do the same for me?'

'I have to talk, Lucy ... must talk'.

'Leave it, Dáithí. You're tiring yourself'.

'I might have another stroke', he gasped, 'and the old ticker ...'

'We're going to be optimistic. The doctors say you are curable. We were so lucky we got you to A&E in time. Besides, I've no intention of being a widow. Come on now, finish off your yoghurt'.

'I need to make a confession'.

'You want a priest? Won't it wait?' she joked.

'Lucy, I've been leading a double life'.

He looked weak and troubled as he struggled for words. She took his hand in hers. She had always admired his hands, the slender fingers and well-shaped nails. She thought they showed sensitivity. She knew men who had fingers like sausages.

'There's someone else', he was saying, 'I've had an affair'.

She couldn't be hearing rightly. 'Did you say an affair?'

He was wandering. She might as well humour him.

'So', she smiled. 'Who was the lucky woman?'

'Sandra'.

'Sandra?'

'You met her. You remember ... at the Christmas social some years ago'.

'I don't think so'.

'We were thrown together ... in a business capacity'.

'You never mentioned her'.

'We are very discreet', he gasped.

Present tense. Let there be no panic. She would play this cool. She had read that the brain was often affected after a stroke. He was fantasising. She remembered her own father, even without a stroke, returning from a spell in hospital and telling her that three nurses had got into the bed with him to test if there was any life in him. But then her father would have been in his early eighties and heading for senility.

The awful voice went on, 'I've been with Sandra for seven years ... we have a little boy. Brian ... started school'.

He was almost animated, a light in his eyes she hadn't seen in years. Holy God! He was telling her the truth. She was mesmerised, frozen in an unspeakable nightmare. This couldn't be happening to her. She began to shake. Dry sobs ripped through her body. She pulled her hand away.

'Please, Lucy, you're the only one I ever loved. I'm so sorry. Forgive me'.

She choked on her sobs. No words would come. Her thoughts hovered like dazed goldfish in a bowl. She would have to get away from his yellow face, his crooked mouth, his pleading. She rose unsteadily and making for the door pulled it closed behind her.

She drew the comfort of the kitchen around her like a blanket and flopped into the cushioned carver. Her head dropped to the table. Had she heard properly? Why, oh why did he do it? How could she have been living in a fool's paradise for so long? She had judged their sex life to have been good, apart from the times he was too fatigued from overwork. She dressed smartly always, not only because she liked to, but he set a great store by appearances. She went to the gym four times a week and even now with all the extra work, she kept the side up. When had things started to go wrong? Unknown to her, he must have had some gripe or he wouldn't have strayed. Or would he? He said they were soul-mates, but she had shared him all these years with another woman. She felt the same terror she had felt as a child when she fell down the stone stairs to the basement and lay in a darkness so dark she couldn't move.

His secrecy and slyness made her stomach churn. How many of the neighbours knew? Maybe everybody did and pitied her. She felt mortified by her trust and gullibility. She thought of the excuses she had made to her parents, her children, her friends. 'Dáithí is a workaholic. You just can't stop him – still at the office'. Or, 'he's at a conference in Killarney this weekend so count us out. Yeah, he's had to go to London unexpectedly'. She remembered her mother's words, 'you are far too accommodating, Lucy, after all you work hard too. His place is with you and the kids at weekends. Believe me, money isn't everything. Assert yourself, girl!'

Of course, money was everything if he had another family in tow. She began to piece together the whole wretched jigsaw.

She heard a banging upstairs. The carpet muffled it somewhat. She had left him his old Croagh Patrick walking stick to thump on the floor with his good arm when he needed her. The ambulance would be here soon to bring him for his therapy. She would say she was feeling unwell and ask the ambulance crew to help him.

She locked herself in the bathroom until they left. She had until five thirty when he returned. She drank a strong cup of coffee and carefully dressed for an appointment with their family doctor at eleven twenty.

As she left the house, she felt that she was walking out on her old life. She saw spears on daffodils, fat buds on the climbing hydrangea, a promise of hope and spring that would be forever grafted in her mind to despair and betrayal.

Dr Manning said she was suffering from burnout. 'You'll have to look after your own health. Now you need some respite and I propose we move Dáithí into a nursing home – say for six weeks. You'll have a rest. Serendipity has a high standard. It is only ten miles away. Pretty expensive, but worth it for a short time. I'll speak to the manageress, Kate Greaney. I hold her in high regard'.

She phoned Seán in Brisbane and told him what she planned. 'Poor you', he said, 'but you must look after your own health and you do know I'd be with you if I could. I'll try and make it by summer'.

She called New York. 'Poor Dad', Muireann said, 'but it's all for the best. He'll come on by leaps and bounds'.

Lastly, she spoke to Dáithí. He looked exhausted after the long day. His eyes, buried in their sockets, avoided hers.

'I've spoken to Dr Manning', she told him. 'He thinks that six weeks in Serendipity would be advisable at this stage. You'll get the best nursing possible and there'll be a room free on Friday'.

'Forgive me', he whispered.

The ambulance arrived at mid-day. She had packed what clothes and toiletries he would need. She herself and her friend, Maureen would follow in the car and see him settled in. She didn't know if she imagined it but she felt he had improved a little in the week since he had made his confession. When he was being wheeled out the door, she could hardly speak with the sadness that engulfed her for them both.

'I'll see you at the nursing home', she said.

'You're doing the right thing, Lucy', Maureen told her as they drove through town. 'None of us knows where you get your strength'.

She was silent, observing the sand bags stacked against the walls of houses and businesses after the recent flooding. The side streets leading down to the river were cut off to traffic. There was more rain forecast. They stopped at the traffic lights.

'Oh, there's Sandra Winters with her little boy. I'm meeting her later for a game'.

Lucy's heart stopped. There must be hundreds of Sandras in the town. Was she going to spend the rest of her life startled every time she heard the name?

'She plays a deadly game of squash. But then, she's at least ten years younger than me. I may pull up my socks tonight'.

'Is that Brian?' Lucy asked.

'That's right. I didn't know you knew each other'.

'I don't. Must have heard it somewhere'. For a moment, Lucy had an impulse to tell her about the wretched affair but banished it from her mind. She wasn't ready yet. She was in shock from actually seeing Sandra and the boy. Not that she would recognise them again. The lights went green before she could stare so she had to keep her eyes on the road.

Serendipity was at the end of a tree-lined avenue. It was an old period residence, the large windows overlooking a well-kept lawn. Brass gleamed on the heavy front door and she could imagine horse-drawn carriages trot to a stop on the gravel. A lavishly-decorated Christmas tree lit up the hall. The ambulance had already arrived.

'Maureen, please don't leave me alone with Dáithí'.

'Are you sure? I was going to take a walk in the grounds'.

'Please stay. It will make it easier to say goodbye'.

'But, it's only till tomorrow. Can't you come back every day?'

'I feel devastated having to do this. I mean putting him in a nursing home so close to Christmas'.

'Of course you do', Maureen hugged her. 'I'll stay with you'.

Once he was gone an enormous loneliness set in. Over and over again, she asked herself if she could forgive him. She thought of all the good times they had shared. One after another they came to argue on his behalf but she was not much good at deluding herself. One bleak fact remained. He betrayed her and his family. That was unforgiveable. She phoned Kate Greaney at Serendipity and said that she had come down with flu, would be confined to bed for at least a week. Kate listened sympathetically and promised to give her daily bulletins on Dáithí's progress. She liked Kate. She was efficient and understanding. You felt there was no problem she couldn't solve. Dáithí would be happy in her care.

'Just make sure', she said, 'that you are clear of all infection before you visit. It would be disastrous if the poor man caught flu'.

At weekends she took to watching Sandra's house, one of a terrace of old houses close to the town centre. She had no trouble locating it once she had Sandra's surname. At first Lucy simply sat in her car with the engine running opposite the house. It had a cherry-red door and a bird-table in the middle of the tiny front garden. That would have been Dáithí's stamp on the place. He liked watching songbirds and was probably teaching the child how to identify the different finches and visitors that came to feed at the table. As the evenings drew in and darkness enveloped her, she parked the car and stared at the house for hours. She saw lights going on and off and once she saw the child, his face pressed to a window, looking down at her. She gaped at his little features through the small binoculars that Dáithí had given her for the theatre. She wasn't a peeping Tom or a stalker. She was just curious. Nevertheless, she felt guilty spying on these people.

Then one Saturday morning as she was about to give up the watch and go shopping, Sandra and Brian came out of the house. Lucy saw that she was no *femme fatale*, but a pretty auburn-haired woman of about forty bringing her child to a games practice. The boy had a sport's bag on his back. She locked the car and followed them to the gates of St Conleth's school. After that she was able to pick the child out in the playground whenever she passed at break time. He seemed to be a happy boy and a good mixer. She wondered if he missed his father or if he had been to the nursing home to see him. There was a chance that the facial paralysis might scare him, although that had improved considerably.

You could have knocked her down with a feather when she answered the doorbell on a wintry Tuesday afternoon and there was Sandra.

'Christ!' she stuttered, '… come in'.

Sandra stared at her but didn't move.

'I was going to make a cup of tea …'

'Tea! God Almighty! Listen to me. Because of who you are, I don't want to go to the Guards. Do you not understand how unnerving it is to have you watching the house night after night?'

'I'm sorry … I didn't realise … It won't happen again'. She could say no more. Her eyes filled with tears as she watched Sandra's pitying look.

'You mentioned tea?'

She nodded and like a sleepwalker led the way to the kitchen.

'Maybe you don't know that Dáithí and I split up over a year ago', Sandra was saying.

She didn't answer but tried to calm herself walking between fridge and table with milk, from cupboard to table with china.

'Please stop and sit down. You should know what's going on'.

Suddenly Lucy felt that she was going stark mad. Did she need to hear any more? Did she need to suffer the steady gaze of this woman on her?

'He begged my forgiveness. I've done my best, but I can't'.

Neither of them drank the tea.

'Dáithí is getting the best of care from his new love', said Sandra with a ghost of a smile.

'New love ... what do you mean?'

'Well, ironically, you didn't know the story or you wouldn't have sent him to Serendipity and the welcoming arms of Kate Greaney'.

'Kate!'

'The same woman!'

'You're having me on'.

'I'm telling you the truth, Lucy'.

'God in Heaven, am I the only one who didn't know? I feel like a proper fool, a simpleton without a bit of wit!'

'Don't be thinking like that. Dáithí was always discreet. He wouldn't let his right hand know what his left was doing'.

'You're telling me!'

Anyway, I heard from Maureen today that Kate is retiring from the job at the beginning of March. Her uncle has left her a house in Umbria in his will'.

'But Dáithí?'

'With the recovery he is making, he'll be with her. A little Italian sun is just what the doctor ordered. Now I must run. Brian is at school waiting for me'.

'One moment, Sandra. Why don't I go with you? It would put his mind at rest to see us together – I mean that I'm not a kidnapper. Do you know what I mean?'

'We'll keep that for another day', she said and let herself out the door.

Translated by the author

COME FLY WITH ME

She twiddled and fiddled with the gold bracelet of her wristwatch, deflecting the impulse to check it yet another time. She knew the hour and the minutes only too well since she was facing the round, white dial of a clock positioned above the emergency exit in the departure lounge which read clearly 21:21. Another thirty minutes before they boarded the plane for Costa Rica.

What in God's name was keeping Dennis? It wasn't fair to leave her here like this minding their hand luggage. She quelled the irritation that rose in her. Just about everything depended on her keeping her cool. After all what more did she expect? She knew that he was full of this pent-up nervous energy and was incapable of staying put for any length of time. Still, a full twelve minutes had passed since he had disappeared in the direction of the toilets. He should have been back by now. Of course he might be looking around the duty-free shops, getting so absorbed that it wouldn't even enter his head to come back and let her off for a while. He had such a detestation of airports that the only way he could combat it was to keep on the move. She imagined his tall whippet-like figure, his eyes darting over jewellery and socks and ties and magazines and booze, striding from counter to counter, sometimes pausing to examine an object but buying nothing.

Kate herself enjoyed airports, hotel lobbies, eateries, in fact anywhere that she could watch people. She found nothing so satisfactory as observing without being observed. Indeed she was close to perfecting her methods of furtive observation. Fleeting dissimulated head movements, her eyes averted from her subject. It was a tricky one and needed practise. Not that she would ever pry. She simply had a broad interest in people.

She pricked up her ears. The American middle-aged man on the other side of her was about to move off and was confiding to his male companion.

'I think that I may have a nervous oesophagus'.

The companion wasn't exactly riveted by this information and continued to check his briefcase.

'Going back to when my Mom fed me some apple-pie and it got stuck in the oesophagus'.

She dropped her eyes. They were passing her by. His voice drifted back to her.

'I notice that my throat contracts involuntarily at times'.

His skin was a greenish shade of sallow. You could say khaki. She was dying to know how the pie became unstuck. The chances were now that she never would.

The woman in the cream trouser suit opposite was oblivious to the little scene. What age was she? Thirty five? Forty? She seemed to be travelling on her own.

Her head was obliquely cast back on the seat emphasing a slight bulge in the centre of her throat. Kate speculated on whether it might be a goitre. When she was a child at primary school she remembered how the teacher used to give out a little white pill daily to each pupil. That was to make up for an iodine deficiency in the water. She wondered if there had been a glacier in the town. In the Ice Age that is. She read somewhere that Marco Polo said that wherever you got glaciers you got goitres. That was because glaciers and flooding washed the iodine from the soil.

The woman straightened herself and stared in Kate's direction. Practising her specialised observation technique, Kate noted that the woman had poppy eyes. That would tie in with her diagnosis alright.

Her fingers automatically flew to her own neck. She was wearing a long pink chiffon scarf and raised the diaphanous fabric, dangling it before her eyes. Her mind at first floated then swam in its lucent ripples and suddenly she was running in the wind and dancing a wild, abandoned Isadora Duncan dance until she was almost airborne. The scarf streaming behind her unexpectedly took on a life of its own reeling and spiralling and tightening around her throat. Kate felt she was choking. Her breath was leaving her in rapid gasps. She was growing fainter and fainter.

'Dennis!' she screamed. Except she didn't really. The scream was inside herself. The Cream Trouser Suit opposite never budged, never heard her rasping breath, never saw a thing.

21:30. The Yank and his friend were coming back. He was silent this time, his mouth wide open, spraying his throat from a small aerosol. Thankfully the attack was over. She felt drained and fluttery inside. How had she knowingly put herself in this ridiculous situation? It was nothing but craziness to have adopted such a passive role. One so incompatible with her true self. Why should she sit here and choke to death with anxiety while her husband was indulging his airport phobia. Ok, ok, take it easy, simmer down, she lulled herself. Patience will pay off in the end. She loosened the scarf around her throat and kicked out at the baggage beneath her feet.

There was no denying he had her trapped. She couldn't leave the luggage and go searching for him because his was much too heavy for her. And talk about her trust! He had both their passports, the tickets, travellers' cheques and indeed the boarding passes all tucked away in a little black leather bag strapped around his middle for safety. He hadn't actually wanted to go on this holiday. It had been her idea entirely. Well somebody had to make some kind of an effort to save their marriage hadn't they? He sure as hell wasn't trying.

She reckoned he had been behaving very oddly for at least a year. Beyond a shadow of doubt, there was another woman. What else? Kate could smell her. She clung like a limpet to every garment he wore. She swam in his eyes. She lay in their bed.

You never heard anything like the unimaginative reasons he gave for his absences from home. They were downright insulting. She got used to the phone ringing with a plethora of excuses.

'Terribly sorry, Kate. I'll be working late on a new contract. Oh, at least until midnight'.

Dennis, give us a break!

'Kate, I've to entertain this chappie from Germany … a new client. It's such a drag'.

Sehr wahrsheinlich! Bloody hell! When he had promised he would go to a film with her. Far worse was the glibness of his call on a Friday.

'Oh, Kate would you ever fold a few shirts for me? I've to spend the weekend in Sligo working with an old and valued client'.

For Christ's sake! Just who did he think he was kidding!

She played for time pretending to believe him. It took her all of a fortnight to formulate her policy. Under no condition would she confront him with her suspicions. That would be playing into his hands. On two occasions she felt sure that he was on the brink of making a confession to her. She knew that she mustn't allow that to happen. If it did there could be no turning back. She must make it as hard as possible for him to leave her. Life without him would be intolerable. It didn't bear thinking about. So, she supposed, she must love him still, or why would she feel like that? She had certainly never loved anyone else. Right. She would be as sweet as honey. Give him no reason to argue or fight. His favourite meals would be hopping on the table when he came home. Definitely no dabbling with pastas or ginger, his particular bugbear. Above all she must never let him know by thought, word, deed or action that she suspected his guilty secret.

She was at nothing. He rejected her at every level, refusing his most favourite stuffed roast chicken and apple tart, spurning her innovative advances in bed when she tried to reach across the shadow woman to him. Well, she thought she was being innovative. She really had nothing to compare her performance with except her friend Cynthia in London who dressed up as a French maid and dragged her man off to

Submission Balls. No way was she going to compete at that level.

The forecast couldn't have been gloomier with their twentieth-wedding anniversary gathering like a trough of low pressure around them. She had a brainwave. She took out the savings she had been collecting for that rainy day and bought two tickets for a package holiday in Costa Rica. In a different environment, set in all the romance of a mountain-top hide-away, she would win him back. If that didn't do the trick they would take boat cruises through channels and lagoons screened with groves of waterpalm. They would cavort in thermal springs and gaze into the living hearts of volcanoes.

Nothing could have prepared her for his reaction when she handed him the tickets in a long white envelope which she had herself decorated with exotic parrots and wanton butterflies cut out from a Sunday newspaper advertisement. He shouted and roared at her most unreasonably. Then he took off with no explanation whatever. Just bolted. She heard the front door bang after him.

That was the first time she experienced a panic attack. And small wonder! She started to suffocate just as surely as if she were being buried alive. She hung on to the edge of the kitchen table willing herself to breathe, to think of wide open spaces and her face was damp with panic.

Dennis had come back that night after the ticket episode. He apologised and confessed that he didn't know what had got into him. Of course he would go to Costa Rica. She smiled to herself in the dark. Things were looking up.

21:40. Another ten minutes. The Cream Trouser Suit was reading now. What the hell did Dennis think he was at cutting it so fine? Her hands were wet with perspiration. She reached into her handbag for a tissue. Supposing he never came back. Simply vanished into thin air. People did you know. My God, she thought, I wouldn't even have the money to make a phone-call.

An airport buggy whirred over the carpet sounding its horn and bearing away three maroon-uniformed airport staff, two young men and a girl, down through the avenue of brightly-lit, duty-free shops. Kate watched the girl's long dark hair flowing behind her. She let herself speculate on Dennis' fancy woman. Was she young? Dark haired like the girl? Or kind of middle aged like themselves? She would bet anything he'd go for the younger model. Not that he was the kind of saturnine hunk who could sweep a young one off her feet. But what if she was looking for a father substitute? She found it hard to picture Dennis as a philanderer. Sure no girl in her right senses would give him a second look. He was cagey as bedamned too. The look before you leap sort. Still facts were facts.

21:43. Thanks be to the Lord God! There he was pacing towards her now. Smiling. He had something in his hand. A red rose. One of those single ones wrapped in cellophane. She felt tears spring to her eyes. Such a really nice gesture from him.

He walked right past her and handed the flower to The Cream Trouser Suit. Kate saw the poppy eyes go all treacley. He turned to her.

'I'm sorry, Kate. I really am, but you wouldn't let me tell you. This is Alison'.

She shuddered with shock and rage. The swine! Had he taken leave of his senses. Introducing her to this cow in the airport of all places! Surely to God he didn't think that she was going to agree to a *ménage a trois*. She struggled to keep calm. Their flight was being announced. She concentrated on every word.

'Will all passengers for San José please proceed to gate number 11'.

Her mind was demented.

'There we go', she croaked.

Dennis looked resolute. 'Goodbye, Kate', he said, and grabbing his hand luggage headed for Gate Number 11, like a cave-man, dragging The Cream Trouser Suit along with him.

Kate had turned to jelly. Her limbs refused to move. She was stuck to the ground like in a nightmare. After what seemed like ages she opened her mouth and screamed.

This time the scream was not inside her. She heard it reverberating around as in slow motion. It rattled furiously amongst the Yank's false teeth. It bounced against the glass display cabinets, setting up sonorous vibrations of crystal and china in the dazzling shops before falling in splintered gasps before the pleadings of the dark-haired girl and the two maroon-uniformed young men who led her and her hand luggage away in the airport buggy, its horn sounding, down through the brightly-lit avenue of duty-free shops.

Translated by the author

A Master of Ring Craft

There was a time when she could look inwards, straight into her own mind and see hillsides tossing with green oats, rolling landscapes under a brilliant blue sky and the sun shining warm on her. She could see children too, laughing from a swing on a chestnut tree. Although she never actually saw their faces or heard them speak, she knew they were laughing and calling her to them.

Recently when she looked inwards, she got dragged into a nightmare country that flailed her like winter and froze her to the earth where she cowered under a tangle of damp leafless trees poised to collapse on her, while a grey fug remorselessly inched in on her threatening suffocation. She had to strain to breathe, to move, to escape. There was something there she didn't want to see. Faceless and dark, it would destroy her.

She tried so hard not to look in. But then curiosity would get the better of her. Maybe the menacing trees were gone? The hateful fug. The faceless thing. She daren't tell Billy. It sounded so childish. Besides Billy and she didn't talk anymore. Words passed between them but you couldn't call that talking. She suspected he was having an affair. Well it was her friend, Nora who got wise to something and tipped her off. Nora could be wrong, of course. She had no actual proof. Or was it that she was holding back information so as not to hurt her? Certainly when she thought about it there were too many committee meetings, Kennel Club meetings, nights spent away from home on business. Did he think she was a fool? He was so sly covering up the evidence. She had taken to sifting through his pockets daily and investigating the car like a detective in search of a hair, an ear ring, a lipstick, a sniff of perfume, anything that would give her proof. But, would it really be proof? After all he could merely be giving a lift to one of his Kennel Club friends. Billy genuinely liked women and women could sense it. Despite this reasoning her searching went on compulsively. So far she'd found nothing but she knew if he was guilty he'd slip up yet. No one could be on guard all the time.

The loudspeaker was announcing the toy dogs' category. She snapped herself back to the present. It was Billy's turn. She looked at him objectively. Talk about loving himself! If he was a bar of chocolate he'd eat himself! There he was off now, swaggering around the ring, putting Princess Yolanda through her paces. Claire couldn't help but smile. He was wearing his lime-green and black spotted waistcoat. She watched him move on feet with evenly-spaced toes. His reflexologist had told him that his toes indicated a balanced perception, a vitality and clarity of thinking. She could feel his confident handling of Yolanda. They moved as one, flowingly, his emotions rippling down the leather lead to the dog, praising her, encouraging her, loving her. He was a master of ring craft and a born showman but he had to be careful to balance the performance and let Yolanda's personality come over to the judges. It was Yolanda who really counted. His job was to bring out the very best in her.

Claire abominated the little bitch. She felt pretty sure that she was Mata Hari in one of her reincarnations. Billy thought this was a weird idea. If she was a reincarnation at all she must be a Buddhist monk. She was utterly still in repose, sitting with her paws crossed and making a little rhythmic noise in her throat which Billy said was her mantra. He could be really dim. He certainly didn't have the balanced perception that his feet indicated. Claire was quite clear on that score. She knew that Yolanda was a professional manipulator and Billy was a sucker for her charms. He couldn't resist those moist seductive eyes, her vampings on the settee, the way she lolled in his lap and insinuated herself into their bed. She out manoeuvred Claire every time and when Billy left the room she'd show herself in her true colours, stripping her teeth and snarling and shaking out the triumphant silk of her hair.

'She's such a cutie. Such a loving creature', Billy said. 'She's the only one who shows me any affection around here'.

Claire didn't trust herself to speak. She inwardly seethed. That was a weakness. She was bad at showing anger. She bottled it up inside her until the fizz went out of it. She was scared of conflict. Scared of losing Billy. She liked their lives to wear a veneer of normality. That was why routine was important to her. Regular meals. The house running smoothly. Paying the bills. The perpetual, repetitive things that wove the two of them together. From them she got a feeling of order and certitude. Everything would be fine between Billy and herself.

Claire knew her dislike of Yolanda was unreasonable. If she had been bitten as a child by a small dog, that might have accounted for her feelings. But she hadn't. She couldn't possibly have suppressed something like that. Nor could it be jealousy. Who in her right mind would be jealous of a dog? Perhaps it wasn't Yolanda's fault? Perhaps, she, Claire, had a problem with all scutty little dogs who sniffed about at ankle level. She knew she liked big noble canines, preferably male, who could look her in the eye. Dogs like Dalmatians or Borzois or Collies or a good decent mongrel who didn't have to be cosseted with baby shampoo and clipped and pruned and sprayed with aftershave. But a beige coloured Pekinese who wore a topknot? An animal in direct competition with her for her husband's affections? An animal who convinced Billy to dye his own hair to match hers? She was crazy not to speak out and tell him she loathed the dog. Crazy not to ask him about his affair and give him an ultimatum.

The dark began to swell inside her again. It was a pinprick at first, then spiralled out like ripples on a pond. She felt she was suffocating, like the goldfish they'd had years ago when the wind blew the window open and knocked it from its bowl on the sill. Claire had found it gasping on the kitchen floor.

'Are you alright dear?' A voice beside her hauled her back.

'Oh yes. Yes thank you'. She heard herself panting.

Now the judges were handling Yolanda, lifting her lips, examining her gums, her teeth, her eyes, her ears.

'You sure you're ok?' said the voice.

'Fine'. She smiled. 'It just got a bit stuffy'.

She watched how Yolanda stood stock still, behaving impeccably throughout the handling as she had been schooled. The judges, two men and a woman looked quite ordinary and down to earth in their tweeds and anoraks. It suddenly struck Claire that Billy looked a bit freaky with his dyed hair, jazzy waistcoat and mincing walk. She didn't want to be a stick-in-the-mud. She believed in letting him be his own person. It wasn't right to inhibit your partner. Well not where dress was concerned. Deceiving and having an affair was quite another matter.

But what about herself? Why was she at a dog show when she'd rather be anywhere else on earth? She did the book-keeping for Mackey's garage and this was her afternoon off. Why in God's name was she spending it here? All she was doing was torturing herself. Billy had no idea she had come. But then that was the whole purpose of the outing. She was doing a spot of detective work. Watching to see if he'd drop guard. So far she could see no particular woman in his company. There were no give away glances. No touches. Perhaps if she and Billy had had a child none of this would have happened. A child would have drawn them closer and there would have been no rubbish about dogs. She would have liked a child, but now at forty five she'd given up hope. More than that he hadn't as much as touched her in the last three years. That was the biggest give away. The sure sign of an affair. They were young enough still to foster if Billy could be persuaded. A child would fill her loneliness. If only their lives didn't have to revolve around the dog shows. Dog show people were not her kind of people. They lived their lives obsessively through their dogs. And they had such power. They actually created the very dogs themselves. She'd seen Billy and his friends studying pedigrees untiringly and arranging the matings that produced the puppies. Still it was sound business. There was good money too in winnings and Yolanda's litter when she had one would bring in a nice bonanza.

Claire slumped in a white plastic chair in the back yard. It was warm for the end of May and she felt quite clammy after her walk in the park with Yolanda. She looked down at her in-turned feet on the concrete tiles. Billy's reflexologist said that turned-in toes indicated shyness and a lack of confidence. She turned her feet out, matching heel to heel. It didn't feel comfortable. Anyway she couldn't win. Out-turned feet indicated a lack of direction and a readiness to be led by others. She'd have to be more assertive. Talk things through with Billy. Stand her ground, take control of her life.

She thought back to the previous evening and Billy's eyes that never looked at her anymore. They seemed to fix themselves somewhere over her left shoulder or was it her right?

'I've to represent the Kennel Club in Belfast tomorrow', he said.

'Oh? Isn't that rather sudden?'

'Well no. I forgot the date actually. Do us a favour, pet, and mind Yolanda'.

'But I can't. I mean I'm working. I'd have to take time off'.

'Sure Mackey's would let you make up the time wouldn't they?'

'I suppose'.

'Look, I'm a bit stuck and Yolanda needs her walkies. Got to have her in peak condition for Sunday'.

Claire thought quickly. If I don't it'll be an excuse for him to ask his fancy woman. Or maybe Gretta. Gretta might even be his fancy woman. She showed more than a little interest in him.

'Where's that dishy husband of yours?' She'd call out to Claire. 'Are you hiding him from me?'

She owned Giovanna Ginervi, a champion King Charles spaniel. She was a widow and one of the flashiest owners at the shows. A stagey platinum blonde, she dressed in powder-blue outfits and gold shoes. She undulated on long narrow feet which indicated that she preferred the aesthetic side of life and loved being pampered. Claire knew she was out of her depth at this level.

'Ok', she said. 'I'll do the needful'.

Yolanda sulked under the skirt of the hedge. Claire ignored her accusing eyes. The dog hadn't wanted to come home. She was having too much fun and attention in the park with children dragging their parents along to admire her.

Claire straightened up in her chair, crossed her legs and drew circles with the big toe of her left foot, ten times one way and then ten the other. She took off her tights and, spacing her tired toes, she noticed the bluish tinge on the skin of her feet. Billy said she should exercise them more. She stretched out and tried to lift a piece of stick off the ground with her bare toes. The reflexologist said that was one of the best exercises. It was too much of an effort. One hand fiddled with Yolanda's identity tag which she had taken off when they'd come in from their walk, intending to polish it. It was a silver rolled-scroll shape with Yolanda's name, address and telephone number engraved on it. A spot of Silvo would make it sparkle. As she rolled it between her fingers, twisting it gently, she felt it loosen at the centre. Strange that she'd cleaned it so often and never realised it actually opened. There was a scrap of paper inside. She prised it out and read, 'Until Belfast, darling. Passionate love and kisses, Cora'.

Good God! Cora! She had the proof, the evidence at last. But Cora? Billy had bought Yolanda from her. She bred pekes and what she didn't know about them wasn't worth knowing. Billy phoned her frequently for advice. She was at least ten years older than him and not at all the *femme fatale* type. A warm, jolly woman who lived in corduroy trousers, she didn't even make Claire's list of suspects. The old witch. And Yolanda was her familiar, infiltrating Claire's home, edging her out of her own bed, stealing her husband. Everything fell suddenly into place. Although she was almost hyperventilating, she wasn't scared anymore. The darkness inside her had a face. She could cope with a face.

Her eyes anchored on Yolanda's. The creature was unnerving. Claire folded up the tiny note and pushed it back in the hollow of the identity tag. It was like burying her knowledge in a grave. She fetched the Silvo from under the stairs and sat in the sun polishing the tag until her fingers were almost raw and small darts of pain stung her wrists. Yolanda didn't resist when she snapped it back on her collar. The dog knew she had her taped and retreated just a little into the shade of the hedge.

Claire walked barefoot into the dim tool shed. It smelt damp and mouldy. Her eyes took seconds to adapt to the dark after the sun outside. She stumbled over Billy's rubber boots before she reached the stepladder and climbed to the top shelf. She felt the coldness of the aluminium steps under the calloused skin of her feet. Her mind was pounding, her eyes refusing to focus. She hoped she wasn't starting a migraine. Her vision was always first to go. She groped for the plastic container of paraquat that she had stashed away after killing off the last of the autumn weeds on the path.

Back in the kitchen, she opened Yolanda's favourite tin of duck and liver. As an afterthought she scooped it onto a gold-rimmed, burgundy-coloured dish that she only ever used for the bread sauce at Christmas. While the dog was eating she'd phone Nora. She could spend the night there. Death should take Yolanda quickly but she didn't intend hanging round to listen to her death rattle.

Darkness was drawing in when she paused with her holdall on the town bridge. The parapet clung to the first of the summer heat. She could feel it comforting under her hands. A small breeze shivered on the skin of the water. She eased the gold wedding ring from her finger and tossed it over the bridge. It made just the tiniest plop and the weeshiest circle that was immediately blotted out in the swift current.

Translated by the author

THE BLUE DANUBE

She leaped up, grabbed the green satin cushion from the couch and she and the cushion whirled round and round the room in a dizzy waltz. It wasn't just any old waltz music that prompted Birdie's sudden impulse. It was *The Blue Danube* that did it. There it was being played on the radio by a full orchestra of soaring violins. It was absolutely irresistible.

When she was young she used to imagine herself dancing until dawn at glittering balls under cascading showers of chandeliers. In Vienna preferably. Vienna was a favourite background for her fantasies because, as she danced, she could feel the great river Danube flowing through the city, licking the foundations of the palaces where she danced, singing under ancient bridges as it wound its way through the tremulous darkness.

Of course she had a dancing partner. Tall and dark, he moved in a fabulous fluidity of steps and half-steps. She knew he was impossibly handsome even though his face was always hidden. Not that she ever wanted to see it. It was of no particular interest to her. His face was quite irrelevant. It was the dance that mattered. She used to love to dance.

When the radio music ended she found that tears were pouring down her face. What in God's name had got into her? Which one of her friends would be barmy enough to dance with a cushion? She must be losing her marbles. She'd never done such a thing before. Never even felt like it. Spontaneity and abandon weren't her line at all. No, she wasn't depressed. Nor was she lonely, even though she lived on her own. Indeed she was happier than most people she knew. She was sensible, balanced and even now, all by herself in the privacy of her sitting room, a little bit embarrassed when she looked at her clammy dancing partner clasped to her bosom. She must have been very light-weight and silly in those Viennese days. But then she was little more than a child and the fantasies no doubt helped her to distance herself from her parents' constant squabbling and fighting.

She plumped up the tear-stained satin. It was quilted long ago by her mother. She knew its plump heart well. It was the last one of many cushions stuffed with feathers plucked from the hens they used to keep in the small town backyard. White of the White Wyandottes; red of the Rhode Island Reds; black of the scarlet-combed black fowl whose name she couldn't remember now.

But in all honesty, she couldn't be crying over dead hens. Didn't she know herself better than that? She caught a glimpse of her reflection in the copper-framed mirror over the mantelpiece. What a holy show she was with her weeping face, some of the wet still shining in the little runnels under her eyes! She wondered about her bone density. It seemed to her that she was evaporating, caving in somewhat. Or maybe her tears were giving a distorted image. Still a couple of layers of fat might have buffered her against the years. She examined the vaguely green face that gazed sourly back at her. Her hair needed colouring again. She looked as old as a bush.

Birdie woke up during the night coughing, but that was nothing unusual. The cigarettes were beginning to take their toll. She groped in the dark for the glass of water she kept on the bedside cabinet. What was unusual was the way she suddenly thought of Leo. Whatever way she raised the glass to her lips, she saw the reddish-gold light of the electric blanket control shimmering through the water and there was Leo's face floating up to her. Leo of all people! She hadn't thought of him in years and here was the blanket light jogging her memory.

A June night. They had gone to the hospital dance together. She knew him quite well so she didn't mind asking him to partner her. They had driven home by the lake. Leo stopped the car. She was immediately apprehensive.

'Did you ever see anything like that moon?' he asked.

His arm stole around her shoulder. She shrugged aside her impatience. Why did he have to go and spoil everything? She could feel herself stiffening. So could he.

'What's wrong?'

'Nothing. I just want us to be friends'.

'Well, we are'.

'I want to leave it like that, if you get my meaning', she said.

'I think you're afraid of me'.

'No. Can't we stay friends? I mean no strings attached?'

'Suit yourself'.

She could see that she had hurt him. But it was better to be honest and not have him getting notions. Her honesty paid off. They both knew where they stood and she was able to phone him any time she needed a dancing partner. She liked ground rules and a structure to her relationships with people. Leo learned that too, even though it took him a while to accept the situation. Sometimes she thought he understood much more about her than she had ever told him. Bar her father she'd never had another man in her life. Leo eventually went to America, but at that stage her dancing days were over. They shouldn't have been, except that almost overnight the dance scene changed and she didn't fancy the newfangled discos, all hot rhythms and throbbing guitars. Leo faded out of her life. In a way he gave up on her. God knows he was persistent enough. He was at her beck and call for ten years.

When she was fifty Birdie had taken early retirement from nursing and come back from London to look after her ageing mother who was living on her own since her husband's death five years previously. She would have been a matron by now if she had stayed. You could say she was a natural delegator and had an unerring sense of the right thing to do in any situation. She often thought that she would have made a good politician. The country was in such a mess with a crowd of mullockers and messers running it.

She didn't even find it strange being back. So much had changed but the sense of familiarity couldn't be erased. She settled down very quickly and made friends. There was Nance and Madge and Etta. Nance, at the end of the terrace, was married to Tommy who was a bit of a slob. Birdie did Nance's big grocery shopping for her every Friday morning. Nance wasn't a good shopper. You could dangle bargains in front of her nose and she wouldn't spot them. Birdie liked helping people and poor Nance was a bit bogged down with five teenagers to look after. Birdie privately thought that Tommy was the equivalent of five more. Not that he was the worst. He had always been decent to her, coming to mend fuses and put in washers or clear the filter in the washing machine.

Nance made a point of having lunch ready for her when she arrived back from the supermarket. She enjoyed those lunches when the two of them could have a nice chat together without interruption since Tommy and the kids didn't come home till evening.

'Are you never lonely, Birdie, since your mother died?' Nance asked her one day.

Birdie was amazed. I mean why would she be lonely? She had everything she wanted in life. A roof over her head. More than that. The view from her front window of the Killeshin hills would take your breath away. She had her pension, her car, her fags, the radio and the telly. And loads of good friends who shared their lives with her. Practically every Sunday she was invited to have lunch in one house or the other. She usually managed to know what was on the weekend menu and if it was roast pork she would wangle an invitation to that particular house. She adored the pig in every shape and form. By lonely she suspected that her friends meant sex-starved. It made her smile.

'Did you never think of marrying, Birdie?'

She wished Nance would lay off the questioning.

'I did not', she laughed. 'You know I never met the man who could keep me in the same style as I could keep myself'.

'Ah, come off it. Couldn't you have kept a man yourself if you'd wanted to?'

Nance made her mad at times. Really mad. She tried to laugh it off.

'When I close my door at night I've nobody to make demands on me, Nance. Nobody to explain myself to and when I go to bed I can go to sleep with nobody to bother me'.

'You're having me on, Birdie'.

But Birdie wasn't. She certainly wasn't. She meant every word.

'Tommy says you're an unclaimed treasure', said Nance.

They both burst out laughing. Birdie was pleased at this description and a glow of happiness flooded her.

'You probably think I'm pure selfish'.

She backtracked a little.

Everybody knew she was the most unselfish person. She was always thinking of ways to help her friends like dogsitting and watering house plants when they were on holidays, shopping, giving their kids' lifts. She preferred the plants and dogs to the kids. They were more easily handled. She never tried to ingratiate herself with young people. They could take her as they found her. Kids preferred honesty. Nobody ever made a fuss of her as a child and she reckoned she was the better for it. And of course she visited Mrs O'Reilly who was an old neighbour and friend of her mother's. Birdie never looked for anything in return for herself but it made it worthwhile when she saw their gratitude.

She couldn't count all the wedding outfits, the confirmation outfits, the graduation clothes, the wallpaper and the curtains she had helped to choose. She had very good taste, even if she said so herself, and she knew what colour flattered each of her friends the most.

'I think you don't like men', Nance said one day, quite bluntly and out of the blue.

What could have put that in her head? She tried to be civil to all her friends' husbands. Even Denis. She put up with him for Madge's sake. Her mother used to say that men were dirty smelly old things and the older they got the worse they got. It gradually dawned on her what that meant. Her mother certainly didn't like men. And with good reason. Her life was one long brawl which only ended with the death of her husband. She had five short years of peace and quiet before death claimed her too. At that stage the last thing she wanted was peace and quiet. She missed the old sparring of a lifetime. Her daughter, much to her frustration, refused to rise to the bait. What a life, thought Birdie. But she was damned if she was going to spill any of the family secrets to Nance.

Birdie had sort of adopted Mrs O'Reilly. Poor old soul. She felt sorry for her. Old age was such a sad thing. She did her shopping for her, brought her clothes to the dry cleaners. Indeed it was some job at times to get the old lady to part with her filthy garments. Birdie would be firm and insistent putting on her best matron's voice. She refused to take no for an answer. She advised her what to eat and what not to eat.

'Oh, no!' Mrs O'Reilly groaned when Birdie produced sardines on toast for her.

'I hate sardines, Birdie, they repeat on me all day long'.

'But they're good for you. You must have two helpings of canned fish a week'.

Mrs O'Reilly eventually gave in. What was the point in arguing? Birdie knew best. When the time came that she could no longer cope on her own, it was Birdie who made the arrangements for her to go into an old folks' home. It was Birdie who locked up the house and went there twice a week to air it and water the leggy geraniums in the sitting-room window.

Nevertheless she was extremely annoyed when the home phoned her to bring in fresh clothes for Mrs O'Reilly. The nerve of them. She hated being taken for granted. Furthermore she saw no gratitude in the old lady's eyes anymore. Could it possibly be the opposite? If she wasn't mistaken Mrs O'Reilly was beginning to resent her, just like her own mother had. Oh, well, it was best to pretend that she didn't notice. She would continue to do the decent thing. Really the poor old woman looked like a witch with her long grey hair straggling down from her bun. She'd bring her to the hairdresser's next week and have the hair cut nice and short. They would have a little treat in the Monument café afterwards. Tea and chocolate eclairs would be really nice. Mrs O'Reilly would like that.

Birdie had a sense of Leo staying with her for days. Leo and the dance. She felt slightly nauseous. She, the sanest of women, began to wonder what was the first sign of madness. Nance said it was talking to yourself. The bad thing was that she could recall Leo's face clearly. Well, that wasn't quite true. It recalled itself.

Up to three days ago it had been a blank, just like the face of her Viennese partner long ago. Now that Leo had managed to dislodge himself from the past he kept turning up at the most unlikely times. Like while she was lying in bed at night thinking over the day, counting all the good turns she had done for her friends and basking in their gratitude. There he was intruding himself into her awareness with a new know-all smirk on his face. She felt like yelling at him to clear off, but it was best to play it cool.

Birdie potted two Busy Lizzie cuttings she would bring down to Madge who had let the last cuttings die by forgetting to water them. She let herself in through Madge's back door which was generally left unlocked, even though Birdie had warned her over and over again to lock up. You simply couldn't be too casual what with all the thugs that were going around these days.

She was on the brink of shouting 'Hi! It's me, Birdie', when she heard raised voices from the next room. Madge and Denis were arguing and blow me if it wasn't about her!

'I tell you I don't want to see that bitch Birdie crunching pork crackling at our Sunday lunch again'.

'Ah, Denis, she's not all bad'.

'And offering her gratuitous advice along with polishing off the apple sauce'.

'The creature's just lonely'.

Oh, God, Birdie thought, I'm not supposed to be hearing this. But she couldn't leave. She needed to know where she stood.

'And I'm sick of her rotten fags'.

The bastard! Denis was such an old woman. After all the times she had put herself out for him. Madge was cowed at this stage, but the monologue continued.

'I never met anyone with such a welcome for herself as Birdie'.

She knew the score. She left the two plants on the draining board and closed the back door softly after her. Madge would get the message. Well, let her stew!

She went home and lit the fire. The evening was turning cold and she heard the wind rising steadily. There was a down draught from the chimney filling the room with smoke. Birdie coughed and lit a cigarette. The phone rang. It was Nance.

'Listen, Birdie. I've brilliant news. I've got that re-training course. Starting Monday morning'.

'I'm delighted for you', Birdie enthused.

But she wasn't too pleased for herself. This would mean the end to her dropping in and out to Nance's place. The end to their little chats and lunches. Birdie knew only too well that Nance would be back in the workplace in six months time.

'I'll keep doing your shopping', she said.

She thought that Nance answered a trifle quickly when she said, 'Not at all. You've done more than enough. I'll be on the spot. I'll do it myself. No problem'.

Birdie had a distinct feeling that she was being closed out. Oh well. If that was the way they wanted it. Even Etta who had never budged anywhere in her entire life was heading off to her daughter in California for three months.

She turned on the radio. Strauss. It was an omen. The music flowed over her. One waltz after the other.

Then *The Blue Danube* again. Leo smiled at her. She looked furtively around her.

'Can I have this dance?' he said.

She didn't want to be too enthusiastic. She leaned forward stubbing out her cigarette slowly and knowingly in the glass ashtray. Then, wordlessly, she rose to her feet.

Translated by the author

The Chocolate Santa

James was a man with problems. There were work problems, family problems, girlfriend problems.

It was 6.30 according to the grandfather clock in the foyer, 6.37 according to the digital watch on his wrist, when the chef walked out. It was Saturday night, a month before Christmas with a hen-party of twenty booked in for 8.30. All tables booked for the night. True the preparation work was done but the basic kitchen staff couldn't cope on its own. James sucked in the insides of his cheeks and chewed on them intently. It was always the same. He felt apoplexy mount in him. How many chefs had he had in the last year? They were a law unto themselves. Temperamental as prima donnas, choosing their time to leave him in the lurch.

He remembered his father and how hard he worked to build up the small hotel with its reputation for good food. He thought of the ungodly hours the man kept, coming in at three or four in the morning to sleep until midday; his mother and the children creeping round so as not to disturb him. There were four of them. James himself, the eldest. His twin sisters, Ann and Mary Rose, five years younger, and Liam, the little brother, three years younger again.

James always knew that he would inherit the hotel. Well not actually inherit it as much as run it for the family. He couldn't be kept away from the buzz, the excitement of the place. The staff spoiled him when he was little, feeding him dainty sandwiches, chocolate cake and macaroons left over from afternoon tea. He was thirty three now and tending to put on weight.

He'd have to call his mother. She was capable, a grand cook and had helped him out before but he felt it wasn't fair to ask her to cater for so many. There was Phyllis too, a local woman who knew the routine. She was willing but would need supervision.

He sighed. Right. He would call his mother. They made a good team. The two of them had kept the business on an even keel when his father had sunk into alcoholism and had to be dispatched to John of God's to dry out. James was seventeen at the time, a good head on his shoulders, and generally accepted Hannah's advice. Still they had had a bit of a disagreement a few days previously when he told her he intended buying a few peacocks to enhance the back lawn. He thought they would look great in wedding photos.

Her eyes snapped open. 'Forget it, James', she said, 'you know the racket they make. They would drive the neighbours stark crazy. Besides, the grounds are simply not big enough for them and our clientele'.

Typical of his mother. Hannah, despite all her good qualities had little imagination.

'Listen, they would be a huge attraction', he argued. 'Kids will love them, want their photos taken with them, collect their feathers and all that'.

'But you don't know the first thing about looking after them. Besides, peacock feathers are unlucky especially if you bring them indoors'.

'Ah, come on, Ma', he laughed, 'when did you start getting superstitious? Listen, I've done my research. They're no bother at all. Easy maintenance. They roost in trees and eat pheasant food'.

Oh God, there should be a law against chefs holding up the show like this! A few hours left. He would agree to abandon the peacock project if Hannah would come and take over. Of course she could have other arrangements made for the night but he felt fairly sure that she would cancel them. The hotel came first. She often told him that responsibility was placed on his shoulders at too young an age. His sisters and brother showed no inclination to get involved. They were content to take whatever hand-outs came their way from the business as if it were their right. There was Ann who was a vet and minting it, still ready for her cut. Mary Rose, married to a builder, herself a teacher and the two of them always with the poor mouth. And Liam, the brilliant one, the eternal student, going from one course to another.

There was no doubt about it, Hannah and he would have to thresh out where his role lay. He was determined that things could not continue as they were. He felt fairly sure that the whole family arrangement was why Louise took off to America. They had known each other since schooldays; had become boyfriend and girlfriend in their teens. For Heaven's sake she was almost his fiancée! They had looked at rings. She said that she would be back in a year's time but he had no guarantee of that. When she left, there were no actual promises exchanged. Just a long time understanding. Nothing to tie either of them. Except he did feel tied. Tied to the hotel and Louise. He wondered at times had Louise become a habit. If they had really loved each other, shouldn't they have been hitched by now? They were both thirty three. Time to settle down.

They had been an item for years at social occasions so he missed her now at his friend's September wedding. Then someone introduced him to Éilís at the end of the meal. She smiled at him. She had amazing green eyes which he later found out were contact lenses. They flirted a little. She was back from Marseille where she told him she'd been a go-go dancer in a nightclub all summer. He was surprised but said nothing.

'So what do you do for a crust', she asked.

'An hotelier', he replied, feeling somewhat dull.

He was unprepared for the enormous interest she showed.

'If ever I win the lottery, I'm going to open a restaurant. That's what I've always dreamed of', she enthused. 'Anyway, I've signed on to do a cookery course in Ballymaloe'.

'Seems a long way from go-go dancing', James said.

'You surely didn't buy that one', she laughed. 'I was actually teaching English to Spanish students'.

Before the evening was over, he had confided in her about Louise.

'How about yourself?' he asked, suddenly anxious to find out if she was free.

She had her problems too – a broken relationship and in no hurry to involve herself in another one although she was an optimist by nature, or so she said.

'He called me a self-enhancer, you know. The bloody nerve of him and his pop psychology'.

'What did he mean by that', James asked.

'Oh, I suppose that I saw the world in a rose-tinted bubble of self-illusions ... protected myself from the uncomfortable'.

'And do you?' he probed.

'Probably. I believe good things will happen. Don't forget I was weaned on the happy-ever-after syndrome. Let's face it, in retrospect he was right. I hadn't read the signs, hadn't seen him for the slime ball he was. I actually had a lucky miss!'

By October, their relationship had changed. Éilís understood that he was tied to the hotel and came to spend the night with him a few times a week. He had done up a few rooms for himself in the attic with plain white walls that contrasted with the ornate wallpapers downstairs. It was his refuge from the hotel. The sort of place you would like to linger in with polished walnut floors, white leather sofas, a shower room with red glass tiles. Louise hated it. He had deliberately not consulted her on it or he would have ended up with a cottagey chintzy look.

Éilís was very agreeable and got on great with his mother. She made no demands on him in contrast to Louise who often felt left out and ignored. She had a sense of style too, albeit somewhat expensive. She liked designer clothes, good jewellery and champagne. She had lost an expensive watch while out sailing with some friends in Baltimore but couldn't claim insurance for some reason James failed to understand. He liked to be seen with her. She managed to look fabulous and was a great hit with the customers whom she chatted up at every opportunity.

Louise wrote a few times – short letters saying she was having a great time and was he still tied to the hotel? Why didn't he come out to her in California and pay a manager to look after the business? She simply couldn't get it into her head that this would be foolhardy. She would never understand.

A fortnight to Christmas and Louise phoned to say she was coming home. James was in a dither. He was fascinated with Éilís – in love with her maybe. Louise was … well … Louise was Louise. It was decision time.

The day was cold, the sky glowering and the staff speculated about snow. Éilís was supposed to have arrived on the evening train. At almost midnight, a taxi pulled up in front of the hotel and there she was clutching something large covered in a fur wrap.

'Merry Christmas, James', she called out 'I've brought you your present. Well, it's a bit early I know'.

'Oh', he said stupidly.

'I'm going to Scotland for Christmas', she said.

'But, you never mentioned … I mean …'

'A last minute invitation. I could hardly refuse it'.

As dramatically as a magician showing off a new trick, she whisked off the fur covering from what she was holding and handed him a box. From the weight, he judged it empty. It was decorated with peafowl on the lid and little holes like he had seen on boxes holding day-old chicks cheeping on a platform at the railway station. There wasn't a peep or a cheep from this box. He carefully opened it and read a gift token card that told him the birds would be his in springtime. Was this a sign of her undying love? He was stunned. Words failed him.

'It's ok', she said, 'Hannah's going to rear them until they are sturdy enough for the hotel'.

James went shopping early the following morning before she woke. He wondered if he should buy her a watch or an engagement ring or both. And he needed something else that would speak for him. He didn't like what he was doing, wasn't even clear on what he was going to buy, but it was the easy way out.

Louise arrived home jetlagged, early on Christmas Eve and went to bed. When she got up somewhat bleary eyed, her mother said apprehensively, 'There's a box for you at the back of the hall, love. A courier brought it. Said it was from James'.

The box lay on the mahogany chest of drawers and in it reclined a huge chocolate Santa. He had the look of an atrophied saint, gaunt from fasting – probably continental with a name like Euphorion or Sigibert rather than Nicholas. Yet Nicholas he was. An enormous white chocolate Santa in a rather plain box with transparent cellophane cover. The most addicted chocoholic would have backed away from the sight. Maybe it was because he was made of white chocolate rather than dark that gave the impression of a corpse in a coffin. There was no touch of red to jolly him up, no hint of Christmas except for some writing on the side of the box proclaiming Chocolate Santa.

Louise turned from it stony faced. The coward! The gutless no-good! He hadn't the courage to tell her to her face that they were through.

Translated by the author

DWAYNE

I was thinking of Dwayne this morning as I drew back the curtains, opened the window, and felt a small breeze lick my arms. I watched how the huge leaves of the chestnut, like the webbed feet of swans, paddled the air and how the creaminess of its candles lit up the garden. When am I not thinking of Dwayne?

When he lived here I never opened the curtains in case the morning light would spill on the bed and disturb his sleep. This morning I deliberately swished the curtains open and closed three times in a row. I might to the casual observer have been testing a faulty pulley. I might have been giving the all-clear signal to a lover patiently waiting outside. In actual fact this was a display of independence and control. Of not having to consider Dwayne. Yet, such is habit that when I turned I half expected to see his form under the duvet, his face vulnerable and innocent in sleep. It is strange how a live absent person can haunt the mind. I can still see him, ear-ringed, in his white suit and white shoes, strolling towards me, ultra casually like that first time almost ten years ago. He was an intruder, singling me out, breaking up our little group.

'Hi Sugar-lips! Wanna dance?' he said.

'Don't. He's a scumbag', my friend Ena hissed.

But I did. That was when I was still at school. A gang of us had gone to the Saturday night disco at the local hotel, the centre of all the action in our town.

'A thing of beauty is a joy forever', said my man, holding me closer than I had ever been held before.

I weighed up his tone of voice, testing it for sarcasm, but decided he was merely trying out what he thought might work. It wasn't the most usual chat-up line but then he was an older man. Older than me by about six years, maybe. He must have been pushing twenty four. All my friends were going out with schoolboys who would have bored me to tears. Dwayne came from the other side of the tracks or to be more exact the top of the town which might as well have been bandit country as far as most of us were concerned.

We were the nice girls from the well-kept houses in the leafy suburbs with two cars in the drive, whose parents knew what they wanted for us, in the same way as we knew what was expected of us; whose mothers made novenas that we would be directed to make the right choice of career in this our final year in school; whose mothers went to daily mass and prayed we would one day find the right kind of professional husband; whose mothers met for coffee to pool their collective gossip; whose mothers went to flower-arranging classes and played serious bridge; whose mothers bought designer clothes in the best boutiques; whose fathers were successful business and professional men; whose fathers gave fat cheques to the church three times a year and ostentatious contributions on a Sunday; whose fathers worked at their golf and talked single figure handicaps and birdies and eagles; and played more golf in Agadir when the weather got bad in Ireland; whose fathers promised us cars of our own if we got high enough grades.

Dwayne seemed to have no constraints. He spoke differently, swaggered with the ease of a Hollywood film star and acted really cool with an acquired American accent mixed with the local argo. I was wary enough, since despite my veneer of sophistication I was as green as the grass and sensed that I was a bit out of my depth.

'Sugar-lips!' scoffed Ena, when we were holding our post-mortem. 'Isn't he the right eejit!'

'He's kinda nice'.

'Give us a break, Louise. He's a smarmy lech'.

'For God's sake, Ena, it was only a couple of dances'.

'Yeah, yeah, sure. But you're seeing him again'.

'Look, I didn't give anything away. He doesn't know the first thing about me. Where I live. Nothing'.

'Don't kid yourself. He knows everything about you. He's a smooth operator. Our Dwaney has his homework done. You'd better be careful, Louise'.

Ena was so smart. So clued in to everybody and everything. But how do you sit in judgment on someone? You could be totally wrong. How can you really know with certainty what a person's motives are?

Dwayne didn't seem as bad as they made out. He seemed decent enough except I knew that I daren't let him hang around our house like my other friends. My mother would think that I shouldn't be let out. He was what she would call a layabout. He freely admitted that school hadn't been his scene so he had left it early and hung around town. He picked up the odd nixer which supplemented the dole and helped him to buy snazz clothes and the occasional holiday in the Canaries.

'Will you cop yourself on, Louise. Yer man never did a nixer in his life'. Ena scoffed. 'More likely he doesn't close his eyes to what falls off the backs of trucks. If you ask me he's a fortune hunter plain and simple!'

Dwayne. We giggled and whispered about him, reckoning his mother must have called him after some hero in *True Romances*. Wayne might have had a certain style but Dwayne was definitely that bit over the top.

I saw him fairly regularly in that final year at school and daydreamed about him just the tiniest bit. I realise now, that even in my daydreaming, I was trying to change him, to mould him into what I wanted him to be instead of ditching the material as unpromising.

Anyway, I had my chances to make a break if I had wanted to. I left school, went away to study marketing and languages and spent a further year working in Spain while I decided what to do with myself. In the end my father persuaded me to come home and join the family business. I was in no way sure that this was what I wanted. Indeed I had promised myself that I wouldn't go back to small town life. Yet here I was deciding to give it a trial run.

Dwayne and I had kept in touch over the years. Well, 'in touch' is a bit of an understatement. I had never really broken with him. I had met up with him in Dublin, in London and in Lourdes of all places. He had taken a cheapo flight which his granny had paid for thinking he was going on the diocesan pilgrimage. I had hired a car and we spent the week in Barcelona together.

During that week, I realised how strong a hold Dwayne had on me. If the truth be admitted he could lay claim to me anytime he wanted. Which, of course, he did when it suited him. Afterwards, I would feel demeaned and used; that I had no guts, no pride.

I think now that Dwayne got as much satisfaction from breaking down small town class systems as he did from sex. Or maybe one stimulated the other. He had quite a convoluted mind. I knew he wanted to marry me but I also knew that he was incapable of fidelity. So our fragmentary affair drifted on from year to year.

Naturally when I came back to the home town, Ena filled me in on all the gossip, that is anything she hadn't already written to me. She didn't spare me where Dwayne was concerned. I got a blow by blow account of his women. As I wasn't anxious to be made a fool of publicly, I gave him a wide berth for a few months. I would not let him two-time me further. But bit by bit he inveigled himself back.

It wasn't so much that I couldn't step away from him. It was more that I couldn't step away from myself. I was a creature of habit who had drifted into him. A bit the way a stream drifts and meanders through flat meadows, joins another stream, scarcely registering the difference and then can't pull back when in cataract country. Perhaps I'm not being fair to myself. I mean presenting myself like someone in a waking trance. In my normal working life I was a confident, efficient person but Dwayne seemed to insidiously master my emotional life leaving me like a thing divided. He had divided me from my family, from most of my friends and from myself.

Shortly after I came back, I became a woman of property. Bought myself a house and took in two lodgers to help pay the mortgage. So much for my fortune! My parents believed in not spoiling me. Dwayne saw it as an ideal pad for himself but at first I was having nothing of it. I wanted a relationship that was based on trust. At this stage I had no illusions about Dwayne. Yet everytime he said to me with practised smoulderiness, 'I need you, angel, and I'm gonna have you', part of me melted into acceptance. Dwayne was certainly a man of action when manoeuvring his comebacks.

My mother, with the backup of her intelligence system, knew about our affair but it was after I'd brought him to a family wedding that she warned me.

'You get this straight, Louise, that layabout will never get one penny of our money. Daddy and I haven't worked our fingers to the bone all our lives to leave the lot to the likes of Dwayne Griffin'.

'So who said anything about marriage or anything permanent?' I bluffed.

I was furious. Who was she to take such an uppity stance? As Dwayne was quick to point out to me. 'Just because your mother got lucky one night in the Ritz herself she thinks she's Lady Muck!'

It was true. My mother and father had met in the old dance hall. She was a shop-girl in a huxter's shop on the edge of town. But that was different. She came from poor but respectable people. My mother flung herself into the business and, if anything, was its guiding light. But what the hell! This was my life. I didn't need an inheritance or a business. I could keep myself and Dwayne too if I chose.

'He's dragging you down with him, Louise', my mother reasoned. 'Can't you see that Daddy and I care about you? All we've ever wanted is what's right for you'.

She saw she was alienating me more and more and changed her tactics. A truce was called. Dwayne's name was never mentioned, but we were a house divided.

Lying in bed, waiting for him to come home nights, I envied the sounds of my lodgers laughing, playing records, having showers. I was getting old. The big thirty looming up. My biological clock ticking away. I had begun to feel restless, tetchy and generally uneasy as if something momentuous and beyond my control was about to happen. The air in the bedroom was heavy and musky. I felt edgy as an animal in oestrus. On such nights I would lean out the window, my thoughts navigating the dark, my ears tuned to a taxi pulling up at the end of the road, to Dwayne's footsteps on the pavement. And night after night for a week he didn't come.

Quite suddenly I began to feel differently. The messing with my life was over. I would break with Dwayne, let the house and move back home with my parents for the time being. The comforting walls of childhood would act as a barrier between him and me and he would never get the money nor the business he coveted.

I phoned my mother to tell her of my plans.

'Oh, Louise, I've just heard. I'm so sorry. I mean I know we've never approved'.

What in God's name was she nattering on about?

'I'm coming round to you straight away'.

'What is it?' I asked falteringly.

'You mean you don't know? It's that Dwayne of yours! I've just heard he's eloped with little Claire Dunne'.

I shuddered. No words would come.

'And Lord love her, she's only sixteen! Are you ok, pet?'

'Yeah. Sure. I'm ok'.

I was trying my best not to throw up on the spot.

'You're well rid of him. You know that?'

'Yeah'.

'You'll forget him in time', she soothed, her tone gentle, solicitous.

'Yeah'.

But it might be hard, I thought, especially if the baby resembles him. I was letting myself think about the life inside me for the first time. Admitting that I was pregnant. I need say nothing to my parents for another month or so and perhaps after all, it would be better to stay in my own house and try to carry on as normally as possible.

Translated by the author

THE GLASS BOOK

Sometimes when I think that I've exorcised my father, he sneaks back when least expected and stands there winking at me from some corner of my memory. I see him again, handsome and laughing like in those days. So unlike my mother who was always cooking and cleaning and tired.

'Why are you forever under my feet?' she'd say. 'Can't you see I'm busy?'

Father and I had a secret. We christened Mother, 'Busy'.

'Let's go walking', he'd say. 'We won't ask Busy'. Or 'Why don't we go over and see the Mangans? Busy would like to be rid of us for a few hours'.

The Mangans lived in a bungalow near the edge of town. Their house was surrounded by trees and shrubs. The front gate had Traveller's Joy trained into an archway over it and in summer the creamy blossoms closed in making the gateway narrow and secret.

Mrs Mangan was a widow with two young children. My father used to say that she was a fine heap of a woman. He said that good neighbours should look after each other. He used to do odd jobs for her like putting in new washers or changing light bulbs.

I liked playing with the Mangan boys. I had no brothers and sisters at home. Mother didn't like the Mangans. I heard Father and her fighting about them.

'For God's sake, Marge, will you keep your voice down'.

But she went on, 'I'm sick to the teeth of you making excuses to visit Annie Mangan'.

'Keep your voice down', replied Father, 'at least for the child's sake'.

'I told you I don't want her going off with you to that place any more', said Mother.

'Well, well, Marge, I do believe you're jealous of Annie Mangan. Don't you know how I feel about you and Catherine? I've never looked at another woman since I met you. C'mon now. Let's see you smile'.

Later I heard Mother say, 'I don't know why I fly off the handle. Maybe I'm in the house too much. Do you know I was thinking of trying for a part-time job now that Catherine is seven'.

'Good stuff', said Father, 'It'll take you out of yourself'.

The visits to the Mangans went on once or twice a week. They had an outhouse where the boys and I played if the weather was wet. It was crammed with cardboard boxes and boards and biscuit tins stuffed with broken beads, ear-rings and the butts of old lipsticks. And there was a little face powder box that was green with a web of black net on it and tiny faded rosebuds in the centre. When you opened it there was a small round mirror inside the lid and the sweet smell of trapped powder.

Once when we were playing there I needed to go to the lavatory and I had to run across the yard to the house. The door was locked. I couldn't get in. I danced up and down in the rain shouting 'Mrs Mangan! Mrs Mangan! I want to go to the lav'.

All was quiet inside. I tried again.

'Daddy! Daddy! Open the door. Please open the door'.

Nobody answered and I wet my pants. I went back to the outhouse and when I looked inside the green lacy box with the rosebuds the mirror got fogged up with my tears.

When it was time to go home my father called, 'Catherine! Come quickly. We'll be late for tea'.

I ran to him whimpering.

'Why did you lock me out? I couldn't get in'.

'Lock you out Catherine!' said Mrs Mangan. 'Such nonsense! The handle's a bit stiff, that's all'.

'You locked me out', I whinged. 'I tried and tried'.

'You're being a silly little girl', said Father. 'We'll be off now Annie. I'll be back next week – to fix the handle'.

He winked at her and she laughed.

'You won't tell Busy will you?' asked Father on the way home.

I was still in the sulks and said nothing.

'She might be cross with us and not let you play with the Mangans anymore. Hey, cuddles, it'll be our secret. Yours and mine'.

I grew used to the locked door and never mentioned it to Mother. I liked having secrets with

Father. He told me jokes too. I told him about Miss
Coffey at school and how her forehead used to plop in
and out like a frog's when she ate her sandwiches.
Then we'd laugh and laugh.

Mother got a part-time job at the newsagents at the
end of O'Neill Street. She used to leave our house key
under the third pot of geraniums at the back door. I let
myself in after school and poured myself a glass of
milk before starting my homework.

One day I saw a blue envelope propped against the
jar of daisies and red poppies that Father and I had
picked the evening before. I was proud of the fact that
I could read grown-up handwriting. I also knew that I
shouldn't read letters not addressed to me, but the
envelope wasn't stuck so I opened it and read:

Dear Marge
This is the hardest thing I ever wrote. Annie
Mangan and I love each other. I'm going away with
her and the boys. I'm really sorry, Davy.

I never heard Mother coming in. My whole body was
shaking with fear.

'Catherine my pet, what's wrong? What's wrong?'

I roared and screamed, 'I hate him. I hate him'.

She prised the crushed letter from my demented
grip and must have read and reread it. All I remember
is her taking me on her knee, her sobs and mine
rocking together till I slept.

I woke up on the couch with the red plaid Foxford
rug we used for picnics tucked round me. Mother was
talking to her friend Carmel.

'I'll never forgive him. Never'.

'Poor Marge', said Carmel, 'you were only far too
good for him. Still, you did suspect something. I mean
you told me yourself'.

'Maybe I did', said Mother, 'but then I suppose I loved him. I wanted to believe him. He had Catherine in love with him too'.

'That's little girls', said Carmel. 'Daft about their daddies!'

'The poor little mite', said Mother. 'She'll never trust another man'.

'She'll get over it', Carmel told her. 'It's you I'm worried about'.

I started to sob and they rushed to console me.

It must have been five years later that another letter was to change our lives again. I watched Mother as she read. Her cheeks grew flushed and when she spoke to me her eyes were very bright.

'Your father wants me – that is, he wants us to take him back. What do you think Catherine?'

I had fantasised for years about him coming home. Now it was clear to me that I didn't want him. Mother was waiting for an answer.

'I don't want him'. I said. 'I only want you'.

'Catherine', she said. 'I think everyone deserves a chance. Will we not give him one chance?'

I thought for a while before I said. 'If that's what you want'.

'That's my girl', she said.

'Where's he anyway?' I asked

'In Scotland', she replied.

'Is he with Mrs Mangan and the boys?'

She nodded.

'And he wants to come back to us?'

'Yes'.

'Does that mean he loves us better?'

'I don't know', she said. 'I just don't know'.

I thought I hated him but my heart jumped with excitement. It would be the same as if he had never gone away. We would be a family again.

Father came back into our lives handsome and smiling and bearing gifts. When Mother said, 'open your present Catherine', I felt shy the way he was watching me.

'You've got so pretty', he smiled, 'I wanted to get you something special. I hope you like it'.

The paper was pink and shiny. I unwrapped it gingerly. Inside was a bed of tissue paper cushioning a glass book which contained perfume. I read the name *Great Expectations*.

'Try some on', he said.

It smelt just like the green box with the black lace and the rosebuds. I couldn't breathe. I was gasping. I thought I would suffocate. It was Mrs Mangan's smell. I ran away from him into the back garden and hid behind the rubbish in the lean-to. I heard their voices at the door.

'She's only just twelve Davy. A bag of sweets would have gone down a treat'.

'I thought she would have been tickled pink with the perfume. Playing at being grown-up you know. That sort of thing'.

My friend Pauline who knew all the town gossip from her big sister, whispered to me that Mrs Mangan had lost her mind with grief when Father left them. She said that she was in a mental hospital.

'And the boys', I asked her, 'what's happening the boys?'

'Oh, their granny is going to look after them and their stepsister'.

I didn't understand the stepsister bit. Pauline was good at explaining. I was so mortified that I hung my head all the way home.

I played with my food that evening until Mother got exasperated.

'Eat your supper, Catherine', she said.

'Is there something wrong, Catherine?' asked Father.

I blurted out Pauline's story. I expected him to be angry but he was convulsed with laughter.

'You're priceless, Catherine', he chuckled, 'simply priceless! What an imagination!'

Mother said nothing. The worry lines between her eyebrows were dark on her white face.

After that Father went out of his way to be nice to me but I was wary.

Four years passed and I got used to him around the place. Mother had a new job as a buyer for a boutique. She was getting on great and had to go to London frequently on business trips. Father came and went as he pleased.

It was June and the midges were gathering under the trees. I remember how the light shone through their see-through wings. When I reached our back door it was open and I heard Mother's voice drifting out.

'Don't do it to us again, Davy. Please don't go away'.

I didn't want to eavesdrop but I stood paralysed on the bottom step.

'Don't go away, Davy. We need you so much'.

I couldn't listen anymore. I hated to hear her beg. Big as I was I managed to squeeze behind the rubbish in the lean-to. My fingers groped for the glass book of perfume I'd abandoned among the empty bottles and jam-jars the time he'd come back.

I squinted through the wooden slats that were crumbling in places and saw him coming down the back steps. He was carrying his brown suitcase buckled together with a thick leather belt. He stopped before the lean-to and rested his case on the wheelbarrow.

'Catherine!' he called.

I wouldn't answer.

'Come out, Catherine, I know you're there'.

I didn't dare breathe. He waited for a moment, half smiling. Then he turned and walked briskly around the corner of the house. The glass book slipped from my tense fingers and smashed on the rough concrete. The nauseating smell of the perfume billowed around me.

It was time to go in to Mother.

MAKING A BREAK

It was on the twentieth anniversary of their marriage that Barry saw with entire clarity that there was simply nothing left to celebrate, unless it was tenacity on both their parts. Life should be a celebration, he thought, not a joyless day-to-day penance. He considered Cathy's tense face opposite him at the breakfast table. She looked spiritual these days, ethereal like some Italian saint. Maria Goretti, perhaps. Maybe it was the way she dressed. The pleated skirts and prim-striped blouses certainly didn't help. They had married when she was only eighteen and he was two years older. He had thrown caution to the winds because he was obsessed with her. Even then he suspected that his had been a one-sided passion. It wasn't that she didn't love him. She simply had no sense of abandon. It didn't seem to matter in those days. Their first five years together were as near idyllic to him as he could have imagined at the time.

They married against the advice of both their families. They were too young. What was the hurry?

Why didn't they at least wait until he had finished his course? But it was the two of them against the world. He tried to dredge up an image of her as she was then. It was useless. The striped yellow and brown milk jug kept intruding.

His eyes furtively watched her movements as she sucked marmalade from her fingers and then with a wet forefinger chased the last crumbs of toast around her plate. He wished she wouldn't do that. She looked up suddenly before he could avert his eyes.

'It'll be nice to eat out this evening. I'll enjoy not cooking'.

She smiled her wan polite smile. He didn't reply. Why the hell do I go on feeding her illusions by doing the right thing? It's time for me to make a break. I must reach out for happiness. He looked startled almost as if he'd spoken aloud.

'You look a bit strained', she said, 'you work too hard'.

He had fed her that line for years. So much so that he nearly believed it himself. He found his work as an accountant monotonous and undemanding. Of course, if he'd had his full qualifications he might have landed a more challenging job. He knew that he never realised his potential. But then he should have been something quite different ... an astronomer or a metereologist. Why he could even be on the telly by now. He could be a household name reading the weather news every night. Better again he might have been a writer. Barry Watson, the novelist, winner of the Whitbread, the Booker, Aer Lingus and *Irish Times* literary awards. He simply never had a chance. Where had his life gone to? Cathy wasn't exactly a help. She gave his writing ambitions no encouragement whatever. That was the basic difference between them.

She was so solid. No, let's face it. She was stolid and unimaginative. If ever he tried to articulate his dreams to her she either decided that he hadn't all his marbles or asked him what was keeping him back. Why didn't he just get down to it?

Talk about sympathy! He felt that deep in the germinant darkness within him lay the seeds of at least two good novels. He had actually made a start on one idea during a slack period at the office. He was so chuffed by the way the prose flowed, he grew quite excited and inadvertently began to read it aloud in ringing tones. He came back to earth rather quickly when Natalie, the manager's secretary, put her head around the door to see what was going on. He didn't mind her curiosity. She was what you would call *simpatico*. He could sense her interest.

'I think you're a bit of a genius, Barry', she had informed him only last week. 'You're certainly different to the dull shower around this place. D'you know something?' she giggled. 'They all think you're an eccentric'.

A fat lot he cared what they thought. He guessed that she was referring to his idea that instead of having the usual office party, they should take the opera train to Waterford, have a meal on the train and see Lucia di Lammermoor. Just as he expected, the social committee squashed the idea. What were they anyway but a bunch of bloody Philistines?

And so when Natalie put her head around the door, he decided to let her in on his secret.

'Come in a moment', he invited and started to explain about the novel.

She butted in enthusiastically.

'You must let me read it when it's finished'.

'Well, actually, Natalie, I'd rather appreciate your opinion at this stage', he replied.

'Ok', she said. 'How about lunch? That is if you're not doing something else'.

He liked her directness. He could never imagine Cathy taking the initiative like that. Cathy was basically such a mouse. Natalie at twenty six belonged to a more confident generation of women.

On their way to lunch, he observed the sly eyes of Fagan and O'Kelly sizing him up. You couldn't even be natural with a woman without those two little shits of clerks keeping tabs on you. Damn the pair of them, forever checking his work in the hopes of catching him out in his calculations. It was so obvious that they were trying to ingratiate themselves with the manager. And they insisted on the most pretentious titles to boost their egos. Fagan decided that he was Head of Regulatory Affairs (Human). The 'Human' in brackets after the title was a great source of mirth to Barry. Poor Fagan. What was he after all but a glorified timekeeper. As for that miserable sleazeball O'Kelly! He wouldn't be a Help Desk Technician except that his tattling to the powers-that-be paid off. Barry used to amuse himself by abbreviating their silly titles and chuckling at their antics as they clawed back. He supposed that he should have asserted himself long ago and let them know who was boss. It would take him all day now to get his figures in order for the board meeting.

Cathy's eyes were on him. He could feel them but he was damned if he'd let on. It drove him crazy the way she studied him as if she were examining a road map. All concentration to avoid a wrong turn. He sensed her feeling for suitable words. It was bad for him to be suppressing his annoyance like this. He should really have it out with her. But what was there to have out? The fact that he found her boring? That he couldn't talk to her anymore? Had she always been the same? Very possibly.

She had never been interested in the great perplexing mysteries of the universe that intrigued him. Mysteries such as ... well black holes or the origins of life.

'Will you come off it, Barry', she used to say and then trot out the usual religious platitudes. She had got herself onto the parish committee and was Father Fennell's right-hand woman. It was Father Timmy this and Father Timmy that. The blue Mazda was often in the driveway when Barry returned from work in the evenings.

The pair of them would be drinking coffee at the kitchen table amidst cumulous clouds of the priest's cigar smoke. Invariably Father Fennell jumped to his feet when he saw him.

'Is that the time, Barry? I'd better head. Must let the man of the house have his meal'.

The priest's wheezy laugh always sounded that bit forced to Barry's ears. He was a stocky, sallow-skinned man with guarded blue eyes. He was probably the same age as himself but he had gone to seed somewhat. Barry noticed the thinning grey hair and the way his stomach sat over his belt. He himself had always looked after his figure and had recently taken to having his hair professionally coloured. Every seven weeks he travelled about twenty miles to a discreet unisex hairdresser in Kilkenny where he wasn't known. Still, the whole parish agreed that the priest was one of the best and that no one knew all the good he did.

'You shouldn't be so rude to Father Timmy', Cathy once said. 'He feels it you know'.

Barry regretted that he had actually encouraged the religious thing in Cathy when he should have stamped it out instantly. There must have been better ways of consoling her when Niall died. The image of their three-year-old son being dragged from the slurry pit swam before his eyes. That was fifteen years ago and Cathy refused to have another child. It was as if her body was a memorial to the small boy.

Outside the kitchen window he could see the cherry tree in a melange of delicate bloom. In the far distance the dark outline of the Killeshin hills was brushed on the morning sky. He tried to erase the image of his son by thinking of the vast mountains of ice piling up at the poles. That had a soothing effect on him, much the same as counting sheep to put yourself to sleep. Next he thought of the birth of planets. He read in the *National Geographic* that they sprang from the dust and gases that surrounded nascent stars.That was good stuff. He would put it into the novel. How miserable and laughable were the antics of Fagan and O'Kelly against such a concept as the energy of the universe!

Cathy's voice intruded apologetically. 'You'll be late for work'.

He pushed back his chair making a squeaky noise on the polished parquet floor.

'It's too early to leave off your vest', she said. 'You know you'll catch cold'.

He hated the outline of a vest under his shirt. He thought it uncool, if not the height of bad taste, but he wasn't going to argue with her now.

'I'll reserve a table for eight thirty', he said briefly and left.

Two days later Natalie came into his office in a twirl of short skirts.

'A crowd of us are going West for the weekend', she said.

'I wonder if you'd like to come? And Cathy of course'.

His heart thumped uncomfortably. He would start hyperventilating if he didn't get a grip on himself. It was now or never. He looked her straight in the eye.

'I'm afraid not', he said. 'Cathy'll be tied up'.

'What a shame', Natalie smiled.

'Would it be out of the question for you to come anyway? It'll be such a laugh'.

'Do I know the crowd?' he asked cagily and was immediately annoyed with himself. He usually tried to project a more devil-may-care image.

'No', she said. 'They're from Dublin. But they're your kind of people. They're a bit of gas'.

He fiddled with his biro, pulling the refill in and out of its case.

'Right. You've sold it to me. I'll go'.

'Fine. That's settled then. You can read me the next few chapters of your novel', she laughed as she closed the door.

The weekend was wonderful. Natalie's friends, two other couples who knew each other well, accepted him immediately. They were fun people and he couldn't help but like them. He found that by Saturday night he was the life and soul of the party and they were making plans for further weekends together. He'd never been unfaithful before except in his thoughts. At first he felt that he couldn't go through with it, but Natalie's manner was so easy. There was none of Cathy's intensity. He let himself be carried along like the creamy froth on the brown trout river that ran beneath their window. That wasn't to say he was mesmerised or passive in any way. He was Adam in a newly-created world. He felt that he had been released from years of erotic inhibitions and repressions, many of them imposed by Cathy. He was afraid that she would think him perverted if his lovemaking took an imaginative turn.

Surprisingly, with Natalie he felt no guilt whatever. The only note of apprehension in the whole weekend was when he thought that she might ask to see some more of the novel. He didn't want to admit to her that he'd run into a dead end. Fortunately she appeared to have forgotten the subject.

On Saturday night he phoned Cathy.

'They're working us off our feet', he told her. 'But the food is great. Fresh salmon and the good life'.

'That's nice', she murmured.

'Sorry I have to dash', he could but hope he sounded natural.

'There's something I want to tell you', she said.

'Can't it hold?' he asked. 'I've really got to fly. We're having another lecture in two minutes'.

'Ok', she replied in a dull voice.

He had decided that the most convincing story for Cathy was that he had to attend a weekend seminar on 'Accountancy-Related Areas'. He thought that appeared sufficiently convincing. She looked at him blankly and seemed to swallow it.

On Sunday when he returned home having rehearsed his act over and over again until it was word-perfect, the house struck him as strange. The darkening clouds were like burnt meringue piped above the roof. He was quite nervous as he turned the key in the lock and called.

'I'm back, Cathy'.

There was no reply. She must be visiting Camilla. Some welcome home! He was ravenous. All that fresh air, not to talk of the activity! A pleased secretive smile at the memory played on his lips. Cathy generally left a casserole in readiness for him if she had to go out. He opened the oven. It was empty. That was a bit much. It wasn't as if he went away all that often. He had reached the curtail step of the stairs, on his way up to dump his bag, when the doorbell rang.

'Camilla', he said surprised as he took in her pink breathlessness. 'Is there something wrong?'

'I'm afraid there is', she said.

'My God! An accident. She's had an accident?'

Camilla opened and closed her mouth like one of those striped tropical fish down in the petshop.

'Is she alive?' he pressed.

'Oh yes, yes. She's fine. You don't have a clue what I'm on about, do you?'

He shook his head.

'I don't quite know how to tell you'.

She drew a deep breath as if about to speak but tantalisingly no words came.

'I have to know, Camilla'.

'It's ... well ... you see, Cathy's run off with Father Timmy'.

Barry felt his chest tighten in pain. He could hardly breathe. Camilla was gabbling on.

'She tried to write you a letter but she couldn't, you see. And then you were pressed for time when you last phoned'.

He looked puzzled. What the hell was Camilla nattering on about?

'The town is agog', she said. 'They just can't take it in. Like who would have imagined Cathy going off with Father Timmy?'

Rage devoured Barry. His knuckles bulged on his clenched fists. He'd wring that bloody sky-pilot's neck. And how dare she deceive him like this and make a laughing stock of him in front of the whole town. The slyness of her manoeuvres sickened him.

'When?' he asked in a choked voice.

'About nine last night. Shortly after you phoned. Look, I don't want to leave you on your own after the shock and all. Will you come over and have a bite with us?'

'No thanks', he said stonily. 'I'll be alright in a minute'.

He wished she would go.

'Oh, one more thing. It's better that you hear it from me'.

Her voice dropped diffidently.

'Cathy's three months pregnant. She says Father Timmy is ecstatic'.

Everything in Barry began to disintegrate. Camilla's face floated in a thousand pieces around him. The voices of the neighbours hissed in his ears. The smirks of Fagan and O'Kelly hurtled past. He was being sucked into a great black voracious hole of the cosmos. Natalie's hands reached helplessly towards him. The last thing he saw before he collapsed in on himself was Cathy's face hovering above him, her eyes sparkling like planets in the evening sky.

THE BANANA BANSHEE

Anyone watching would have sworn I was giving Val my undivided attention. My friend Fidelma, an inveterate matchmaker, had just introduced us. Her choice of men for me usually left me cold and this was no exception. I was actually drifting in and out of listening as if I was coming out of an anaesthetic. The evening was a bit of a yawn and it took all my willpower not to retreat into myself, to ponder the futility of life and to count stars shooting against the velvety darkness of my brain. Val's voice jolted me back like a dig in the ribs.

'Did you know that it was the Pilgrim Fathers themselves who invented it?'

What on earth was he on about?

'I'm telling you now. They used to make a concoction of pine needles and the chippings of walnut trees. Oh yes. The cocktail's sure come a long way!'

I laughed with relief. Encouraged, he leaned closer towards me.

'Here, have a slurp of my Alabama Fog-cutter. It's the drop of vermouth that makes the difference'.

The idea of a cocktail hour had been dreamed up by Fidelma as a fund-raiser for the local musical society, trying to recoup losses on its most recent production *Hello Dolly*. She had modelled the evening on the Plaza Hotel, New York in the 1930s, which was why I was standing there, all six feet of me, *gottied* up in short black silk, ballooning out in layers of fringed chiffon and thinking only of escape.

'So, what are you drinking?'

Wow! There was actually a gap in his knowledge!

'Banana Banshee', I said sourly, licking what tasted like a lemony-orange froth from my lips.

'Can I have a taste?'

I handed him my swizzle stick knowing he couldn't possibly taste much.

'Mmmmm ...', he sucked, 'nice tension there between the ingredients'.

He scanned me up and down. He had an aquiline nose that gave him a greedy look as if he wanted to possess me. In what sense I wasn't sure, but I had these vibes that lodged somewhere in my guts. I clung to my glass as if it were a strong stake anchoring me.

'What do you do?' Val questioned.

'I'm an artist', I said evasively.

'Me too'.

'What kind?'

'Oh, groovy. Contemporary. I express bodies and feelings and how they relate to each other'.

'Christ!' I said under my breath. What kind of a nerd had I been saddled with! I stood up as if summoned by an unheard bell, said I had to go and like Cinderella made a bolt for it.

I didn't see or think of Val for another six weeks. Not till Fidelma came round one evening after work.

'Hey, Lynn', she said, 'we're having a 60s night for the musical society on Saturday. Say you'll come'.

I groaned audibly. I was suffering.

'Val'll be there. Isn't he drop-dead-gorgeous and he really fancies you!'

'I can't', I blustered. 'I'm off to the country to visit the folks'.

I could already see spring outside the train window, fields of winter corn flashing past, a dusting of catkins on the trees, my folks making a fuss of me. I didn't need man-hassle. How could I, after Martin ditched me almost at the altar and took off for Australia with a girl he had known a mere few months.

Fidelma refused to listen to me.

'You're cloistering yourself. All work and no play. You might as well be a bloody nun. You'd have more sport in a convent. Cop yourself on girl! Your folks will still be there next week'.

I yielded, painted butterflies on my big toes, put on a purple mini, a long string of green glass beads swinging down to my stomach and headed for the fundraiser.

When I spotted Val, I wondered was it him at all. He had a more highly evolved look about him than I remembered and seemed less overpowering, merging with the crowd, listening, rather than holding forth. To my surprise, I found myself hoping he would come in my direction, but when he did as if on cue, I didn't let on I saw him.

'Well, if it isn't the Banana Banshee herself!' he whispered.

The ice in my glass shivered slightly as my eyes swam into those greedy ones trying to possess me. That's when I knew he was still quintessentially him. He certainly looked different without the thirties gear.

'How's the art going?' he asked knowingly. I realised Fidelma had split on me, so I stretched out my sandaled feet. The glorious butterflies looked as if they were about to take off. I had studied their every movement in the Butterfly Centre in Carraroe. Watched them as pupae hanging from a twig in the over-heated glasshouse; sketched the first flutterings of wings, their flight, and now the captured stillness on my toenails. Stillness and patience was what it was about. If you work in miniature as I do, you must do your homework with precision as well as imagination.

'You're a manicurist?' Val was enquiring.

'A nail-artist', I corrected. 'Flowers, butterflies, cartoon characters, whatever turns you on'.

I had no notion of elaborating.

'I think we've a lot in common', he said smiling.

From that night in the Plaza onwards, Fidelma was forever begging me to give him a chance. It was on account of her and our friendship that I decided not to run him. There was no way I was bowled over.

Within two months Val and I had become an item. I never fell in love with anyone quicker. And that brought me back to the old chestnut, of speculating about love and puzzling whether it was possible for a man to love a woman without trying to possess her. Love is a discovery, one of the other. My experience had always been that the less you give away the better since familiarity invariably breeds contempt. That is why as a rule of thumb I keep an escape route at the ready, an emotional trapdoor that I can drop through at will. No man on earth was going to hurt me again. What I didn't realise was that by being evasive and trying to conceal myself, I was in fact revealing far too much to Val and that by moving quickly he had battened down my trapdoor before my very eyes. I might have been one of my painted butterflies. There was no escape. I tried not to panic.

Little and all as I gave away, I was conscious that Val gave less. He was ostensibly open, loving, frank, talkative. It was clear that he was very taken with my height. When he invited me for the first time to his workshop in Kilkenny, I was flattered but not prepared for what lay ahead. Bear in mind that I thought I was visiting some class of art gallery, but this place smelled as antiseptic as a hospital. It was obvious from the inks, the needles, the general equipment, that my loved one was a tattooist. Sketches of the Sacred Heart and all kinds of religious images mingled with anchors and roses and snakes on the four walls. I could have murdered Fidelma. The bitch! Of course she knew. I felt such a fool.

'So, you express bodies and feelings and how they relate to each other', I said with as much sarcasm as I could muster when I found my voice.

'Do you have a problem with that?' he said.

Of course I didn't, but yet I did. I'd thought that Val might have wanted me as an artist's model; that I might have become famous like the wife of the French artist Pierre Bonnard who painted his wife languishing in the bath or draped against the garden vegetation.

I had met the real Val at last. Gone was the poseur and know-all. He explained how he listened to music as he worked; how he used the rhythm of the music, transferring it to his subjects. He demonstrated the amount of preparation work that went into his pieces; how he realised his responsibility to his customers whose chosen designs were as much an expression of themselves as they were of him, the artist.

I think I was two months pregnant when I next visited the workshop. I looked squarely into the liquid eyes of the Sacred Heart, Padre Pio, St Christopher and a pantheon of unrecognisable saints. Did priests and nuns really wear the holy ones under their garments? There was Cú Chulainn too and Mona Lisa, and St George and the Dragon. Val himself was wearing a yellow cutaway singlet which showed off to perfection a bunch of bright bananas on his left forearm and my name under them. His assistant had designed it under Val's direction. I began to laugh hysterically. He loved me. I thought how angry and defensive I had grown after the Martin experience. Now I had renewed confidence in the world. Val and I had a kind of cerem ony.

'Does it hurt?' I whispered, looking at the needles and inks.

He tenderly swabbed my upper-arm close to the shoulder with disinfectant and deftly traced on it a single banana, his own name in the folds of a leaf. He worked gently, competently. I didn't feel a thing and the tattoo was very pretty, really much nicer than a ring.

Fidelma was gobsmacked when I showed her.

'Jesus, Lynn, you've tied yourself up good and proper! Why didn't you use one of those transfer tattoos? I never thought you had it in you. There was no need to go over the top'.

But there was. She didn't understand at all.

She continued, 'I can tell you I wouldn't do it ... not for Val, nor any other man'.

'I'm not tied in any way', I said proudly. I wasn't going to say anything further.

'Would you give over', she laughed, 'Where else have you got a tattoo?'

Once we had a home together, Val developed a passion for gardening. Not on a big scale, you know, but in window boxes. The following spring, he had parrot tulips that would take the sight from your eyes. He was fascinated by their abandon and flamboyance. He looked at me longingly. Oh, I wasn't mistaken. It was my skin he coveted. Six feet of prime canvas. But it was mine. In the beginning, I was reluctant, but in the end, I gave in. I let him tattoo a yellow-red parrot tulip down my backbone. I lay on my belly, thinking of the child inside me and taking comfort and happiness from Val's hands drawing fine lines on my skin, the swirl of feathered petals swimming between my shoulders.

As for my own art, I shared it with him. Lovingly, meticulously I adorned his finger and toenails with wild flowers and insects of every kind. On the first anniversary of our meeting, I pierced the third nail of his left hand and hooked in a thin gold ring. Fidelma said that was different since it wasn't permanent.

By the time the baby was due for delivery, my body was a riot of colour. All of Val's personal feelings for me and our child were transferred to my skin. My gynaecologist's eyes widened somewhat when she examined my abdomen for the first time. Beneath her fingers, a serpent writhed under an apple tree and Adam was half hidden in Eve's tangled hair.

It was a wonderful picture. Eve's face resembled mine. Adam's face was Val's.

'Why did you do such a thing?' the doctor questioned.

'My husband', I said, 'he's an artist'.

'Good God! And you allowed this? You do realise, Lynn, that tattoos like this are irreversible?' she murmured.

I understood. When I saw her worried face it got me thinking once again of love and commitment and possession. Val was so obsessed with the living canvas of my body, would he ditch me when the canvas was full, or would he need me as his life's masterpiece? I got a chilly little feeling in the pit of my stomach when I faced the fact that our sharing was not quite equal. He could erase my nail-paintings with a ball of cotton wool soaked in polish remover. In his mind, love and the realisation of his artistic ambitions were one. I prefer to think that he loves me in his own way. However, I decided not to hand over any more canvas for the time being.

The baby was born. She is now three years old. Sometimes I see her father look at her longingly, greedily as if he can't get enough of her. I see her eyes swimming into his. I keep a sharp eye on them. These days he is teaching her to draw little yellow bananas.

Translated by the author

About the Author

Deirdre Brennan is a bilingual writer of poetry, short stories and drama. Born in Dublin, she spent most of her youth in Clonmel and Thurles. She studied English and Latin at UCD followed by a H.Dip. in Education. She has lived in Carlow for many years and was a founder member of Éigse Carlow Arts Festival in 1978 and later of Comhaltas Ceoltóirí in Carlow. She is the recipient of many prizes including Poetry Ireland Choice of the Year (1989), *THE SHOp* poetry translation award (2002), Oireachtas awards for poetry and radio drama and a Listowel Writers Week short story award (1996). Her stories and drama in English have been broadcast on national radio and on Cork Campus radio. She has published ten collections of poetry to date, the most recent, *Hidden Places : Scáthán Eile* (Arlen House, 2011). Her stories in Irish were published as *An Banana Bean Sí agus Scéalta Eile* (Coiscéim, 2009). Her work has been widely anthologised, most recently in *Twisted Truths: Stories from the Irish* selected by Brian Ó Conchubhair with a forward by Colm Tóibín (Cló Iar-Chonnacht, 2011).

Staying Thin for Daddy is her first collection of short stories in English.